# *All I Want for Christmas*

## *Lynn Emery*

# MORE BOOKS BY LYNN EMERY

Between Dusk and Dawn
A Darker Shade of Midnight
Best Enemies
Night Magic
Happy New Year, Baby
Gotta Get Next To You
Tell Me Something Good
Good Woman Blues
Soulful Strut
After All
A Time To Love
One Love

Chapter 1


Controlled chaos surrounded Nedra in the convention hall turned mega dining room. Under most circumstances she would be horrified as she loved order and hated surprises, but instead she felt satisfaction. Dozens of volunteers sat around six of the large, round tables. Nedra was pleased with their attitude. There was not a trouble maker in the bunch, if she didn't count Mr. Earl, who grumbled about everything. There were still two hours to go until the doors opened to the hundreds of people expected for the community Thanksgiving dinner. Most of the volunteers preparing the food had taken a short break to hear one last organizational speech.

As Nedra scanned the crowd, an unfamiliar face made her pause. Actually, it was his body that she noticed. Tall and muscular, the newcomer wore black pants and a white shirt, just like the others, but he was also wearing a black vest over the top, which made him look like a waiter from a very upscale restaurant. Nedra, who made it her business to become familiar with all of the volunteers, was certain she would have remembered that face – and body. The booming voice of her boss tugged her attention away from the man.

"Hello there. Good to see you. Hi, Paul and Clare. Good to see you." Constable Rodney 'Rod' Davidson beamed as he shook hands and slapped shoulders in good humor.

As the executive director of Holiday Hospitality, the constable worked the crowd and greeted a group of prominent people who helped out every year. He would be giving a motivational speech to everyone and Nedra was quite happy to let him take the spotlight. As second in command, standing on the sidelines smiling and nodding suited her just fine. That way she could blend in and slip out to the kitchen area where the other volunteers were keeping things moving.

Constable Davidson, or 'Big Chief' as he was affectionately called, cleared his throat dramatically and drew up to his full five foot ten inches. "Good morning and happy Thanksgiving. I'm truly grateful that so many of you willingly sacrificed time with your loved ones this holiday. What better way to show love and thanks for all we have by giving to those who have not. Twenty years ago, when our annual Baton Rouge Holiday Hospitality Dinner started, just a couple dozen folks showed up. Our event has grown tremendously because of wonderful people like you. Now we feed hundreds, physically and spiritually. Working together, we've shared a lot of love.

"This year is going to be better than ever. I speak for the entire planning board when I say a truly heartfelt thanks to all. Now I know you're eager to get to work and my second in command, Ms. Nedra Wallace, is probably looking at the clock, willing me to wrap up this speech." Constable Davidson paused with a smile and waited for the laughter to die away. "So we'll end with a brief prayer from Father Braddock of St. James Cathedral."

Nedra paused for a second when she heard her name and blushed as several city dignitaries smiled at her. Still, she continued down the hall that led to the kitchen area. A tall, thin man moved through the crowd and fell in step beside her. Dwayne Grover was one of the mayor's top two assistants and had his finger on the pulse of the entire parish; something he repeatedly told Nedra or any other woman he thought might be impressed. Dwayne wore a snappy, charcoal-gray suit and spit-shined, matching leather shoes. Nedra was not surprised that he had managed to wriggle out of breaking a sweat as a volunteer.

"He does love an audience, huh?" Dwayne said.

"Hmm." Nedra knew something was coming, and he wouldn't need much encouragement to dish.

She was right on target. Dwayne glanced around to make sure they were alone before speaking. "I heard Rod is seriously considering a run for the Louisiana Senate next year."

"Oh, did you?" Nedra kept her voice and expression neutral.

"You're doing a good job acting like you don't know. C'mon, you're probably printing up campaign posters as we speak." Dwayne chuckled.

"City employees aren't allowed to take part in political campaigns as I'm sure you know," she replied mildly.

Dwayne snorted. "Yeah, like top staff don't know how to get around that nuisance rule."

Nedra ignored his obvious attempt to spark a reaction. She veered off to her right and into a large room filled with huge aluminum pots of food. Men and women wearing aprons and hair nets bustled around, making sure the meal was warming.

"Before you ask, we've got it all under control. The turkeys and dressing are across the way," said Alice

Faye, without breaking her rhythm of stirring what was cooking and adjusting pot lids. In charge of the kitchen detail, she usually worked in the food service division at Louisiana State University, where she managed two large student cafeterias.

"Thanks, Alice. You're an angel in an apron," said Nedra. She grinned at her and winked. "I'd hug you, but I want you to keep working."

"We rockin' and rollin' up in here," a man chimed in.

"Yeah, Nedra, Alice Faye cracks the whip as hard as you do," another man wisecracked.

"You guys make it easy," Nedra replied.

Dwayne gave them the thumbs up. "Yeah, you folks are doing great. Keep it up."

Nedra resisted the urge to roll her eyes or make a sarcastic remark. Dwayne had his uses, much as she hated to admit it. His political and social connections had helped the committee to attract high-profile national sponsors this year. His ability to network was part of the reason he had landed so close to the mayor president of East Baton Rouge Parish. So, Nedra didn't object when Dwayne followed her down the hall to her next stop.

The smell of roasted, smoked meat floated past as they moved. One half of the next room was taken up by a long counter space, perfect for large chafing dishes. Nedra nodded as Dwayne kept talking. He only paused when she approached a couple of volunteers to gain updates. Then Nedra went back down another hall where two level, wheeled carts were lined up.

"Everything seems to be set up just fine," she said. "We'll have fifteen people in a line, loading plates and placing them on the cart. The volunteer servers will then take the carts and place the food on tables. Another set of people will pour ice tea and water for our guests." Nedra took a deep breath and fanned her face. "So far, so good."

"You're doing a phenomenal job," Dwayne said, moving a bit too close.

"Thanks," Nedra replied, placing some distance between them. She pretended to double-check the carts in the hallway for sturdiness.

Dwayne adjusted his tie as he spotted some reporters and videographers from two local television stations. "Everybody knows you're the real brains," he said to Nedra. "Rod is just a figurehead sucking up all the glory. He wangled his way into the honorary title of executive director and official host to get free media face time. The mayor shouldn't have let him get away with that one. Elections are won on feel-good crap like this."

"We'd like to think this 'feel-good crap' is truly meaningful," Nedra shot back in irritation.

"You know what I mean," Dwayne replied, turning back to her as the journalists headed off in a different direction. "Listen, why don't we get together after you're through here?"

"Hey, sorry to interrupt, but..." said Alice Faye, suddenly appearing and placing a hand on Nedra's arm.

She spun to face the older woman in gratitude for the interruption. "No, no. What do you need? We've got a whole bunch of priorities here."

Alice Faye shot a quick glance at Dwayne and a light flipped on in her wise, brown eyes. She gave a sharp nod and looked back at Nedra. "For sure. Less than two hours 'til show time."

"Right, right, I'll catch you later, Nedra," said Dwayne, scurrying off. He had spotted the mayor, surrounded by reporters, heading towards another section of the large, L-shaped kitchen.

"Thank you, I..." Her voice trailed off as the tall, handsome stranger from earlier popped into view a few feet away.

"No problem. Oh, he's the reason I stopped you," explained Alice, waving the man over. "Hey, come over here, son. Yeah, you!"

Mister tall, dark and delicious strolled over. Nedra thought his wide grin turned up the heat better than any of the commercial stoves. He had a long-legged stride that made him move like a dancer and his slender, neat mustache changed her mind about disliking facial hair on a man. His long dreadlocks were pulled back into a hair net, which was required when working in the food prep area.

Nedra's first impression had been correct: the man had a lithe, strong body that filled out his shirt, vest and pants quite nicely; just enough to inspire a quick fantasy in any female hungry for a man. Like Nedra! She shook her head to regain control of herself and was pleased to find him looking at her shoulder-length hair in appreciation.

"Carlos, this is the HBIC – head babe in charge," announced Alice Faye, chuckling at her own joke. "Nedra is chief of operations for our holiday dinner. Nedra, Carlos Jacobs stepped up to volunteer at the last minute. Just in time because Mrs. Stevens had to bow out. Her arthritis kicked up."

"Nice to meet you," Nedra blurted out, taking a step closer to accept the man's extended hand. She blinked at the warmth as his fingers wrapped around hers.

"Good meeting you as well. You run quite an event here. Well done." Carlos dipped his head, as though bestowing approval reserved for only a lucky few.

Nedra smiled back at him. Her surroundings faded as though someone had hit the mute button and she was lost for a minute.

Alice Faye cleared her throat loudly, and Nedra snapped back to the real world. She blinked a few times and then blushed with chagrin. "Thanks, but we're a

7

team," she said. "With fabulous people like Alice Faye, my job is super easy." Nedra tried not to feel as big a fool as she probably looked.

Alice Faye glanced from Nedra to Carlos and then backed away. "I just realized I have to find Bill and make sure all of the containers of dressing arrived. Oh, and the guys were late bringing those big cans of green peas, so I'm going to make sure they're in the pots and heating up."

Nedra panicked, not wanting to make an even bigger fool of herself. After all, she had a bad track record. She always fell hard for tall, dark strangers with sexy lips and eyes smoky with promised passion. Carlos Jacobs fitted that description perfectly. Her last three romantic disasters flashed before her eyes. "Wait for me! I could help," she suggested.

Alice Faye turned to her. "No, give Carlos the quick and dirty version of the orientation. You've got time. He's already been a huge help. Carlos made a chart of the food assembly line." She then gave Nedra a wink that seemed to say, "Go get him, girl."

*Is every older female in my life a matchmaker now?* Nedra suppressed a groan, recovered herself, and faced Mr. Invitation to Get in Big Trouble. She stiffened her spine against Carlos' obvious appeal and squelched her tendency to fantasize about Happily Ever After. In the past she had been knocked back to reality too many times.

"So, Carlos..." Nedra stumbled on the first down.

The man grabbed the ball and was back in charge. "I've heard a little about Holiday Hospitality, but to be honest I haven't done volunteer work since college at Tulane."

Good looking and college educated. Nedra ticked off two boxes on the 'must have' list inside her head. She let a little starch out of her spine. "Let's go to my temporary office, aka the broom closet."

His rich laughter caused more heads to turn their way. "A great executive can lead from anywhere and still get results."

Nedra walked beside him, feeling a glow from that liquid gold voice. "Are you bucking for a new employee bonus?"

Carlos laughed again. "I'm willing to earn one, for sure."

"Oh, my," Nedra whispered, taking a deep breath at the sensual reference in his words. Somehow she managed not to melt into a puddle, but kept walking until they reached her temporary command center. Carlos' powerful smile made his full lips even more delectable up close and Nedra felt a power surge of attraction. She swung her office door wide open and pointed to a chair beside the small table that served as her desk.

Carlos glanced at his wristwatch. "We could do this another time if you're pressed. I won't need the full history to be a waiter."

Nedra tried not to drop to her knees and beg him to stick around. "Everything seems under control; besides it won't take long. Here's a brochure you can read later, in case you want to volunteer again."

"Sounds good, so tell me more," replied Carlos, folding the paper and sticking it into the inside pocket of his vest. Sitting down in the chair, he leaned back.

"It's not complicated really," said Nedra. "Holiday Hospitality was started twenty years ago by my boss' predecessor, Constable Theo Grady. He was a sweet, giving man who is greatly missed. Anyway, Mr. T. organized the first dinner."

Carlos grinned. "They actually called him that?"

"Yeah, Constable Grady got a kick out of the nickname. He'd even do his own imitation of the famous

Mr. T." Nedra laughed. *Who could have guessed that I'd be enjoying my volunteer efforts this much?*

"Wish I'd met him. He sounds like a fun guy," Carlos said.

"He was. Mr. T. wanted to serve folks who couldn't afford the traditional, fancy Christmas dinner, but he didn't require that people be poor or homeless. A lot of lonely folks with no family spend the holidays alone, especially the elderly, so we don't have any income requirements or question who shows up. This is a true community outreach for everyone."

"Holiday hospitality in its truest form," said Carlos with a nod. "Poor people don't feel singled out either, for once."

"You get the concept. Even better, people with money who would otherwise be lonely get to share a warm, welcoming dinner. The idea was so popular that the following year, Mr. T. added Thanksgiving. I volunteered to be operations chief for the 2012 Thanksgiving dinner. At Christmas I'll just be a server, like you."

"What, no cooking?" Carlos's rich voice teased her.

"Oh, I can whip up some good food. I mean..." Nedra backed away from what could be interpreted as a come on.

"I enjoy cooking a bit myself, not that I'm an expert by any means. But I'm willing to learn." Carlos leaned forward.

Now Nedra had no doubts at all. Carlos had deftly and gracefully indicated his interest. He wasn't pushy or conceited like Dwayne, who assumed most women would leap at the chance to bask in his glory. Instead, Carlos had a classy way of extending an invitation to take things to the next level.

"An eager student is half the battle," Nedra said.

"I'm aways open to new things," Carlos replied, and

leaned back again. "Like volunteer work."

Nedra regained control of her breathing in order to speak. "I'll make a note of that. Ahem, anyway, back to the history lesson. Both dinners are so large that there are two separate committees. And that's it. Short and sweet."

"I appreciate the perspective; makes my participation more meaningful." Carlos flashed that glorious smile once more.

"Well, um, we try to make Holiday Hospitality rewarding for everyone, and that includes the volunteers," Nedra replied, standing. She teetered for a second on her three-inch heel pumps.

Carlos stood and placed a large hand under her elbow. His touch sent cold chills and a flush of warmth all over her body. *This man could be contributing to global warming with the heat he can turn up.* While Nedra worked on recovering from the flash fire of lust, he worked against her by stepping closer.

"Careful. We need capable leadership," Carlos said, as he steadied her. His face came closer.

"I should change into the ballet flats I brought with me. So much for looking cute," replied Nedra. She gazed into his hot chocolate-brown eyes and sighed. *Is it magic or did I intentionally tilt my head in preparation to taste those delicious-looking lips?*

"Is this your office number written on the brochure?" Carlos asked.

"That's my cell number, just in case the volunteers have an emergency during a dinner. I usually only give it to the section leaders," Nedra murmured, captured by the full curve of his lips.

"May I keep it, even though I'm not a section leader?"

"Sure, since you're so new at this," Nedra answered promptly, and then cleared her throat.

"Hey, Nedra, Rod is asking about..."

Dwayne seemed to materialize out of nowhere. He stopped talking, stared at Nedra and then glanced down to where Carlos was still holding her arm. "They need all volunteer servers out front," he added.

Nedra straightened. "We were discussing the dinner. Carlos stepped in at the last minute to help out."

"Carlos Jacobs. Nice to meet you, Dwayne," said Carlos, offering his hand.

"We've met?" Dwayne gave him a distant, chilly glance as he shook his hand briefly.

Carlos smoothly ignored Dwayne's pointed looks at Nedra for an explanation, and replied, "My mother arranged for the mayor to be the luncheon speaker at the last Martinet Society public issues forum."

Dwayne shifted his focus back to Carlos. "Your mother is...?"

"Judge Yvonne Jacobs, Division C of the Nineteenth Judicial Court. I attended the forum and you were introduced. Plus I've seen you on the news a couple of times. The mayor gets high marks for his efficient team." Carlos nodded.

"Umm, thanks." Dwayne seemed torn between warming to the ego stroke and bristling with male competition. His ego won as a smile turned his mouth up. "Well, we do get it done. Not just me, of course. We certainly appreciate Judge Jacobs' support."

"I'll let her know," Carlos replied. "You're right. I should report to my battle station. I'll see you later, Nedra." He touched her elbow lightly with the tips of his tapered fingers and moved on.

"Sure." Nedra enjoyed the view as Carlos walked away, unaware that she'd brushed past Dwayne to watch him stride down the hall.

"Damn, I leave you alone for a minute and you're all up on the help," Dwayne quipped with an edge to his tone.

"I wasn't 'up on him', as you put it, and why did you come looking for me again?" she clipped back.

"Rod wanted someone to check on the progress back here, and I said I would."

Dwayne guided Nedra back into her office and closed the door.

"Whoa! What do you think you're doing?" she asked, putting up a palm just in time to keep the door from closing completely.

"Look, my situation is complicated, but you know I have feelings for you, girl." Dwayne tried to take a step forward, but stopped when Nedra pointed a forefinger at him.

"Complicated as in married with two kids, so let's clear this up – I'm not interested in being your secret fling." Nedra picked up her tablet computer and crossed her arms, pressing it against her chest.

"I told you, we're separated. I mean, Gwynne and I have already talked about it. She'll be moving out after New Year's. C'mon baby..."

"You're married. End of discussion," replied Nedra in a level, but firm voice.

"So that's it? You've already moved on to him?" he asked, jerking a thumb in the direction that Carlos had taken.

"I didn't have to 'move on' to anywhere. There was nothing between us, and I don't have to discuss my personal life with you." Nedra squinted at him. Dwayne definitely inspired a temperature spike, but it was anger instead of attraction.

"Fine, just don't pretend you weren't into to me for a minute before mama's boy showed up." He moistened his lips with the tip of his tongue. "Remember the fundraiser last month at the Shaw Center for the Arts?"

Nedra thought back to the first of October when she

attended a swanky party to raise funds for the local community arts organization. After about an hour, she had a nice buzz from downing glasses of fine wine. Dwayne's flattery had chased away her 'forty and still single' blues and at some point they ended up alone on the balcony. She let him kiss her once, but luckily another couple stumbled out there. Frantically pawing each other, the couple tried to claim the same dark corner. All four had stammered embarrassed apologies, avoided looking at each other directly, and gone back inside.

"I made a wrong decision after too much wine," said Nedra. "That's all it was, a momentary lapse. It won't happen again. Now I need to get back to work."

She glared as Dwayne smirked to show his skepticism. He stepped aside and opened the door wider, answering, "Whatever you want to tell yourself, Nedra."

She started to walk out, but paused in front of him. "Oh, and by the way, Dwayne…"

He glanced down at her breasts and back up again. "Yes?"

"A real gentleman wouldn't have brought up that incident," she replied, walking off from him.

"I didn't say... Nedra, wait a minute!" Dwayne called after her, but gave up when she didn't slow down.

****

"Everything is smooth, boss lady," said Alice Faye as Nedra re-entered the kitchen. She wiped her brow with a napkin and huffed.

"Sounds great. The carts are lined up, all the food arrived?" Nedra tapped the screen of her tablet. "Turkey, dressing, green peas, rolls?"

"Check on all that, plus the pecan pies and pans of bread pudding for dessert are all laid out." Alice Faye was about to say more, but stopped as she glanced over Nedra's shoulder. "Dwayne looks like he wants to talk; to you, not me, definitely not me."

"No, he doesn't," she replied without looking up.

"He's gone. I think he'll get the message soon." Alice Faye gave Nedra's shoulder a pat.

"I think he already has," Nedra shot back. "Jerk."

She was about to call Dwayne a few other choice names when Carlos appeared from around a corner. The judge's son moved heavy pots and pans as if he was used to serving others, yet Nedra knew he came from a privileged upbringing. Unlike Dwayne, Carlos didn't radiate conceit and entitlement.

Alice Faye followed Nedra's gaze. "He fits right in."

"Yes, a nice fit for sure," she mumbled, more to herself than in response to Alice Faye.

## Chapter 2

Carlos finished working by six-thirty that evening and headed over to his parents' home. Thanks to precision timing, the Holiday Hospitality dinner had begun serving a little before noon. By three o'clock, they had finished handing out the plates, except for a few late stragglers. 'To-go' plates took care of any leftovers and the clean-up went like clockwork. Overall, a very efficient operation.

Carlos had tried to keep close to Nedra Wallace as much as possible, without making it too obvious. The woman wasn't just window dressing; she got her hands dirty and worked alongside the other volunteers. She had changed into slim, denim pants and a big, comfortable LSU T-shirt towards the end. Not only was she cute, but Nedra had leadership skills. Her fine curves were obvious, even beneath that oversized T-shirt covering her hips. Carlos smiled at the way Ms. Wallace managed to be no-nonsense, all business and sexy at the same time.

He arrived at his parents' home after a twenty-minute drive from downtown. He turned off his CD player and parked in the circular driveway. His younger brother's BMW 335i and his sister's Buick Enclave showed they were still there. Carlos cut the engine to his steel-blue Acura MDX and sighed. He hoped there would be less drama than usual, but no fireworks at a Jacobs family dinner was always a long shot. He strode to the side entrance of the house and used his key. The security system chimed as a signal that the door had been opened.

"Hey baby, happy Thanksgiving. I'm just leaving," said Margie, the part-time housekeeper, as he walked in. She air-kissed him on the cheek and brushed by.

"Whoa! Happy turkey day to you, too," Carlos said, catching her by the arm. He pecked her on the right cheek. "You're running out of here like the kitchen is on fire."

"Nope, the fire is in the dining room. I came by and brought my red velvet cake in time for dessert. Now I'm outta here. Besides, my house is still full of relatives watching football." Margie was about to go on when raised voices sounded in the background. "Goodbye and good luck."

Carlos sighed for the second time and watched her go. "Please, take me with you. Adopt me. Please."

Margie chuckled. "You're always welcome, but we both know you better show your face in there."

"Yeah, warm family fun awaits," he muttered.

Carlos walked down the short hall, through the kitchen and into the formal dining room. His parents sat at either end of a long, oval table. Trey, his younger brother by two years, sat on one side with his son, Keith. Carlos' younger sister, Brianne, sat on the other side of the table with her husband and their two children. In contrast to the smiles that Carlos had just left behind, no one at this dinner table looked happy.

"Good evening, everyone," Carlos announced and was greeted in return. Then his family got back to their regularly scheduled program.

"Have a seat, son," his mother said, waving at the empty chair to her left. She turned her attention back to Carlos's father. "Stay for cake and visit with your grandchildren."

"Business doesn't stop for holidays, Yvonne." Jefferson Williams Jacobs, 'JW' to family and friends, drained his wine glass. The slice of cake on his saucer was untouched.

"Granddaddy, can I have your cake?" asked Brianne's daughter, Cheyenne, giving him her most fetching smile.

"Cheyenne, one piece of cake is enough," Yvonne said sharply.

The girl looked down. "Yes, ma'am."

"You're sweet enough without more sugar," JW replied. He picked up his granddaughter's plump little hand and kissed it.

"Let's go play that new game daddy bought me. C'mon," suggested Keith. He grabbed his ten-year-old cousin's hand and pulled her from her chair.

"Me, too," said Lincoln, Jr., Brianne's youngest. He seemed thrilled to seize any chance to escape the table. He was tall for a seven-year-old boy and already into sports.

"Not without giving me a hug first, young lady," JW said to Cheyenne in a pretend gruff voice.

"Love you," the girl whispered to him, as though it was a treasured secret shared between them. Then she raced after her eleven-year-old cousin and younger brother.

JW waited until the children had disappeared into the large family room down the hallway before turning back to his wife. "Stop making that child feel bad about herself. You and Brianne watch like hawks every time she takes a bite of food."

"Daddy, I'm trying to get Shy to eat healthy. That baby fat, as you like to call it, might not go away otherwise." Brianne patted her lips with one of her mother's fine linen napkins.

Her husband, Lincoln, drained his wine glass dry and followed his father-in-law's lead. "Leave the kid alone, Bree. You've put on a few pounds and nobody's hounding you about it."

"Oh no you didn't." Brianne's light-brown eyes flashed and for a few seconds she looked like her mother.

"Lincoln, apologize to Bree. She gained those pounds giving you two beautiful children," Yvonne snapped.

"Linc is talking to *his* wife about *his* daughter. He didn't ask for, nor does he need to take a poll before doing so," JW clipped. He pushed his chair back and stood. "Now, if you'll excuse me, I'm going to check on that shipment."

"You will not leave this house," Yvonne said firmly. "At the very least, our grandchildren deserve some of your precious time.

"I didn't say I was leaving the house, Yvonne," JW shot back. "My inventory staff worked half a day today and entered things in the computer. I'll be in my office."

"I wasn't insulting you, babe. You're fine as ever," reassured Lincoln. He gave Brianne a quick kiss.

She raised an eyebrow at him. "Sweet talker! Are you ready for some football?"

"See, Carlos, I have the perfect wife – nice butt and loves football." Lincoln winked at Brianne as they both stood and started down the hallway.

"I'll bring the beer," Trey offered.

"You've had enough to drink. You're driving, remember?" Yvonne stated firmly and stared hard at him.

Trey sighed, but said nothing.

"I'll check in on the kids and then watch a few minutes of the game before I do some work," JW said. He gave his wife a quick, pointed look before turning his attention to Carlos. "Hey, son."

"Happy Thanksgiving to all," Carlos said in a dry tone. He shook his father's hand and then walked the length of the table to kiss his mother. "I can't stay long."

"Yeah, I hear that waiting tables is rough," Trey teased.

Carlos gave him a thin smile in return. "I had a great

time as a matter of fact. I met some really nice, down-to-earth people."

"They say Rod organizes a wonderful event for those people," Yvonne said.

"Actually, Nedra Wallace does the hard work. She had that dinner organized and running like clockwork." Carlos pointed to his father's uneaten slice of cake and sat in the empty chair that had been left for him.

"Take it," said JW, sitting down. He pointed at Trey. "And you can wipe that smirk off your face."

"I believe I met her once," Carlos' mother replied, watching him chew a bit of the cake. "I'm not sure we know her people, JW."

"Humph," was her husband's only reply. "So, Carlos, you thought about what we discussed?"

Carlos chewed slowly for a few seconds and then sipped from the water glass left at his place setting. "We didn't 'discuss' it. You talked as if the decision had been made. My answer is the same. I'm not selling my business and working for you."

"Detailing the cars of drug dealers and scruffy small-time pimps is a bad business move," JW retorted. "At least consider relocating."

Carlos cleared his throat and avoided his mother's gaze for the moment. "Stop stereotyping people just because they live in a poor neighborhood."

"Priceless Thanksgiving dinner conversation," Trey quipped. "I'm going to play with the kids."

"I sure hope you didn't buy Keith one of those profanity filled, violent games," Yvonne called after him.

"Of course I did, mom. Kids learn a lot from experiencing real life," Trey tossed back over his shoulder.

"I'm going to my office," announced JW, standing. He followed Trey out of the dining room.

Yvonne stared daggers at their retreating backs and then drank some of her wine. "Your father loves to keep to a schedule, even during family time."

Carlos sighed. "Margie's red velvet cake is a taste of heaven. As for dad, he's regular in his habits and it's made him successful, even through the recession."

"Oh yes, your daddy is consistent. He sticks by his commitments: same wife for thirty-seven years and the same mistress for seven years." Yvonne raised her glass in a mock toast and then drained the rest of the wine.

"Mother, I don't think..."

"Sorry, dear. Scratch that last remark from your memory." Yvonne laughed and refilled her glass. "I won't ruin our family holiday gathering."

"Hmm." Carlos ate some more cake without looking at her.

Yvonne sipped her wine. "So, you were very impressed by this Nedra Wallace? She's Rod's assistant at the constable's office. They must work very *closely* together."

"What's that supposed to mean?" Carlos snapped.

"I wasn't implying any such thing. I only meant that she has a responsible position under him." Yvonne studied her son in silence for several moments.

Carlos ignored the subtle double entendre. He put his fork down and stood. "I'll help you clear the table and load the dishwasher."

"No, dear," she replied. "Margie cleared up almost everything and even packed up the leftovers. Brianne and Trey have their bags. I'll fix one for you, too."

Yvonne rose slowly to her full, commanding height of five foot eight. She liked to joke that dressed in three-inch heels and judge's robes, she could scare the pants off most attorneys.

Carlos thought she looked regal, but she swayed slightly for a few seconds. *Too much wine.* "No, you don't have to do that," he said. "Join the others for the game." Standing, he put an arm around her shoulders.

"I could use some alone time after all this family bonding," Yvonne replied, patting his cheek and picking up her wine glass.

"Okay," Carlos said, feeling slightly guilty as he watched her walk off to the kitchen.

In all honesty, he had offered to let her join the family so that *he* could escape. He guessed that more drama was on the way. Watching his mother, he felt sad for her. Brianne and Lincoln were happy, for now. Every year Brianne became more like their mother. Trey seemed to live on sarcasm and dissatisfaction. As for their father...? Carlos shook his head and started for the den. Then he remembered the warm, genuine smile of a curvaceous woman with milk-chocolate skin. He walked into the formal living room for some privacy and took out his cell phone.

****

Nedra fussed with her hair one last time before stepping out of her Honda Accord. The cool fall air caused her to button her black, suede jacket all the way up. The Fish Bowl was a popular restaurant, specializing in seafood, and there she was meeting Carlos, the son of the prominent Jacobs couple. She hoped it wasn't a mistake. They only met two days earlier.

Carlos' call on Thanksgiving night had been a delightful surprise to Nedra and caused a sensation at her family dinner. Her older sister would not stop talking about it, and her mother had frowned and said she should have introduced him by now. Nedra grimaced at the memory of the ensuing commotion, caused by the three women trying to get in on her personal business, but she had stood firm. That only meant her oldest sister,

Jarae, would play detective and try to sniff out the facts.

Nedra wanted to keep Carlos as her own little secret until she knew where things were going. The last thing she needed to hear was another chorus of "tick-tock" as they all reminded her that she wasn't getting any younger. At forty, she was the only one without any children.

Nedra entered The Fish Bowl and left those bleak thoughts outside. *I'm just here to have a nice dinner and maybe get to know him better. If he's a creep, I've got my own transportation home.* She smiled at the approaching waitress. "I'm meeting someone. I'm early, so I'll take a table and wait."

"Of course." The waitress started to lead her towards a table and then paused.

Nedra followed her gaze to find Carlos walking towards them. She tried not to blurt out the first thing that popped into her head, which was how absolutely scrumptious the man looked. Carlos was wearing a forest-green, V-neck sweater over dark-brown slacks. His half-smile made him even more handsome, if that were possible. Nedra wasn't the only woman who noticed.

"Hello there. I sat at the bar and watched some sports news. You look wonderful," Carlos said, placing a hand under her arm.

"Hi, and thank you," Nedra replied.

*He's early for our first date, starts off with a compliment and he's gorgeous. Oh yeah, I'm already having a nice evening. Unless he grows a hump in his back and starts to drool, I'm taking this man home!*

Nedra used the time it took for them to get seated in a cozy booth to exercise some self-control. Still, she couldn't help but give a victory smile to a few women who stared.

The waitress glanced at her. "Can I get you

something to drink?"

"I'll have spring water with a slice of lime, if possible," said Nedra.

"Sir?"

"Pinot Bianco for me," Carlos replied.

The waitress nodded and hurried off.

He glanced at Nedra. "Just small sips since I'm driving."

"Otherwise I'll have to take you home," she answered and then clamped her lips shut. She almost added, "Drink up, baby. Drink right on up!"

"I promise you that I don't make a habit of drinking and getting behind the wheel," he assured her. "So, now we're getting to know each other right off the bat."

Nedra relaxed against the imitation, red-leather back of the bench. "We already know some things. For example, you know I'm a little obsessive compulsive about being organized, and I arrive early for appointments."

"I wouldn't call it compulsive and being early is a great habit in a woman. Guys hate to sit around waiting." Carlos grinned. "What do you know about me?"

"You know how to work hard and be part of a team. If you've got an ego, you checked it at the door at the holiday dinner. You seem to enjoy helping others." Nedra broke off when the waitress returned with their drinks and took their orders. "So, how did I do?" she asked when the woman had left.

Carlos gazed at her for a time, as though seriously thinking over her words. Then he smiled. "I did like helping people to enjoy themselves, and I was working hard because I've never been a waiter before. You didn't see my slip-ups."

"Ah, nothing major. You got some desserts mixed and dropped a plate. No harm done." Nedra shrugged when his eyes widened. "My job was to be on top of things. For a first-timer, you did just fine. Most of the volunteers aren't professional at serving."

Carlos gazed at her in silence. "So you expected me to have an ego?"

"Your mother is a judge and your father was the first black man to own a Big Burger restaurant franchise in this city. He eventually expanded to a total of six cities, with two in Mississippi, before selling them and opening a contract clean-up business." Nedra stopped short. "Sorry, that sounds like I've hired a private detective to investigate you, which I didn't," she added quickly.

"Let me take a guess. Dwayne Grover gave you a complete rundown on me and my family, in between trying to get next to you." Carlos laughed at Nedra's scowl at the mention of the man.

"How'd you know?" she asked and laughed with him.

"I watched him watching you. Besides, Dwayne makes it his specialty to know who's who and what's what. He was like your shadow when he wasn't chatting up movers, shakers and reporters," Carlos replied.

"You know him well, I see. He does love schmoozing with powerbrokers," said Nedra, leaning back as the waitress arrived with their food.

"Steamed scallops for the lady and grilled red fish for you, sir. Enjoy." The waitress flashed a smile before she scurried to the next table.

"I'm sure you move in the same circles socially. Your mother also knows my boss," Nedra continued.

Judge Yvonne Jacobs had a reputation for being temperamental and the worst kind of snob. She was believed to have a queen-sized chip on her shoulder because she had grown up poor in Dry Prong, Louisiana, without a pot to pee in. People with any sense knew not to bring up that subject. Yvonne's last political opponent, and several lawyers who had been in her

25

court, found that out the hard way.

Nedra dug into her salad and considered what she was getting into. *This is just dinner.* It was time to remind herself not to go too fast.

"Yes, my parents have a lot of friends," Carlos said mildly.

Nedra speared a scallop with her fork and then paused. "Your parents know appointed officials, doctors, bank presidents and more. Don't be so modest."

"True, but they're just people." Carlos cleared his throat. "And they are their friends, not mine."

"I see." Nedra raised her eyebrows as she gazed at him and decided to let it go. "So, you know what I do for a living. What's your profession?"

"I own a couple of car detail shops. Saved and scraped up my pennies to open the first one seven years ago. My father promised to match my funds and help me to get a business loan, but I had to prove I had discipline," he replied, in between eating some of his fish.

Nedra smiled at him. "So you can handle a dollar and like being your own boss."

He laughed. "Some say I have a problem with authority, but yes, I like the charge of taking a risk and making it work."

"A true entrepreneur, following in your daddy's footsteps." She grinned at him and savored her scallop.

"Only when it comes to owning my business," Carlos said sharply. "We're different in a lot of other ways."

"Alrighty, then," added Nedra and drank some water.

Carlos seemed to relax and then smiled. "You know, it's the usual father and son conflict. We always swear we're not going to be like our parents."

"Mothers and daughters have the same issues; older

sisters and younger sisters, too," she said with a nod. "I promised myself that I wouldn't make the same mistakes I watched them make."

"Whoa, this is getting a little heavy for our first date. I wanted us to have fun, not relive family drama." Carlos placed a hand on her arm. "Sorry."

Nedra's body responded to his touch, practically screaming for more 'fun' with him, but in private. "It's okay. I'm having a good time. Not that we're going to rush anything. I mean, like go back to my place."

Dead silence stretched for several moments.

Carlos cleared his throat. "I don't expect you to. By fun, all I meant was enjoying some good conversation and getting acquainted. Despite my reputation, I'm not looking for a quickie with you, Nedra."

"No, no. I had a huge brain fart, blurting out that stupid thing about my place," she replied. "Maybe I'll have some wine. Sheesh."

Carlos laughed and signaled the waitress, who responded promptly. "Bring another wine glass please. My friend would like to taste mine."

"That's our best, too," replied the waitress with a smile. Moments later she returned and set the wine on the table.

"Thanks." Carlos carefully poured about half of his glass into Nedra's. Then he gazed at her and leaned forward. "I think you'll like it."

Nedra felt another flash of heat. "Looks really, really good." She sipped the wine as she continued to look into his eyes. "Hmm, hints of apricot and pear, with a smoky undertone. Wonderful flavor."

Carlos nodded slowly. "You're a wine enthusiast. Something else we have in common. When can I see you again?"

*Get your mind straight, girl. Don't make the same old mistake you've made before. No taking him home too soon, only to have him go 'poof!' like a ghost. You're better than that, and you deserve more.* Nedra repeated to herself the mantra of her support group of girlfriends, all trying to recover from being 'desperate females' on the hunt for Mr. Right.

She sipped some more wine, savoring the taste as it slid down her throat. Her reply would be a kind of test, but would Carlos get impatient or annoyed? He seemed content to let her decide what she wanted; a man willing to wait for something of value. Nedra's emotions swelled. This felt different from her recent dates with men who had expected her to prove *she* was worthy of *their* attention.

"Well, next week will be hectic at work after the holidays," she answered. "I may have to work late for the first few days."

"So, let's get together on Sunday afternoon for coffee and dessert after dinner. L'auberge Casino has a great little cafe with a river view." Carlos held up one palm, dramatically. "Truth time…"

"Oh?" Nedra's stomach tightened. Was this the first bad news to prove this date was too good to be true?

"My mother expects me for Sunday dinner at least once a month," he explained. "I haven't been to her house once this month and I missed most of Thanksgiving dinner, but if Sunday is too soon..?"

"No, I'd like that," she replied, and sighed inwardly. "I wouldn't want you to disappoint Judge Jacobs. I have a feeling that future family dinners would be tense."

"You have no idea," Carlos replied and gave a grunt.

"Oh, I think I do. 'Ain't no drama like family drama." Nedra shook her head.

Carlos tilted his head to one side. "We're going to have a lot to talk about. I feel comfortable talking to you. Most times women try to pump me for information on my parents. They rush to get all my stats, including what

I'm worth."

"Get out of here! No woman is bold enough to ask about your money, surely?" She asked, grinning.

"True story; one woman asked my net worth. She was an accountant and in a hurry. Tick tock." Carlos tapped his wristwatch and laughed.

"Oh Lord, do I know that phrase. Being forty with no kids, my mother..." Nedra stopped short. "I'm older than you."

Carlos waved away the difference and shrugged. "Forty isn't that much older than thirty-five."

"Forty," Nedra repeated in a low tone.

Doesn't matter," Carlos put his hand on her arm again. "Believe me."

Nedra nodded and they kept talking... for hours. They stayed in the restaurant until almost midnight. Carlos joked that the management would flick the lights to get rid of them.

When they parted, he hugged her with just enough warmth, but no suggestive groping. During her ride home, Nedra felt like she was floating. She replayed the wonderful evening in her head all night. *Carlos Jacobs might not be the one, but he was sure doing everything just right for now.*

## Chapter 3

The following Tuesday after work, Nedra met with her youngest sister, Gaylynn, and two friends, Maida and Imani, at a little grocery and cafe. All four of them worked in city government, but in different departments. Capitol Grocery Store was popular with city employees and young professionals. Many lawyers could be found there, especially when court cases dragged on into the evening hours.

Nedra and Maida had been friends since high school. Maida had two kids and was divorced, while Gaylynn had two kids and a live-in boyfriend, and Imani had been engaged three times, but no wedding. They ordered a big platter of appetizers: hot wings, tiny meatballs, cheese sticks, two types of dip and some potato skins. Talk about the trials and triumphs at their various offices soon died away, and turned to their social lives, which usually meant dating.

"Let's go to the Upstage Theatre on Saturday night," suggested Imani. "They're putting on their first whodunit play. My friend's cousin wrote the script." She patted her ruby red lips with a dainty series of motions. Her stained napkins looked bloody.

"I love a good mystery. Let me see if I can get a babysitter. Mama has been acting all funny, so I can't depend on her." Maida grimaced.

"You mean she's got her own life and doesn't want you dumping the little darlings on her," Imani retorted. She laughed and then ducked as Maida pretended to aim a swat at her head.

"Yeah, the nerve of her having a man and a social calendar," Nedra chimed in. "Look, Miss Eleanor deserves some fun."

"Whoa, whoa! Get off my back, please," Maida said.

"I want Mama to be happy. I also don't want her to get hurt by some slick-talking church deacon. He looks shady to me."

"Your mama was dealing with men before you arrived on this earth. Let Mrs. Tullier have her fun. Besides, if it doesn't work out, she can handle it," Gaylynn replied, waving her hand. "Our mamas are made of stuff that these young girls today need to model."

"Including us?" Maida reached for a potato skin and scooped up some of the dip.

Imani nodded. "We could do better following their lead."

"Well, they're human, like anybody else. They made mistakes too," Nedra put in. She had grown up convinced that her own mother nagged her late father too much.

"I didn't say they were perfect, but take my mother: she didn't let men walk all over her," Imani said.

Nedra, Gaylynn and Maida exchanged glances. Maida cleared her throat loudly and Nedra took a big sip of her strawberry lemonade to keep from commenting. Gaylynn had no such hesitance. Imani's mother had four ex-husbands and counting.

"Baby, ordering men around and giving ultimatums doesn't work very well," Gaylynn answered, giving Maida and Nedra another glance.

"Y'all can stop giving each other the side eye. You have to be two steps ahead of a man." Imani waved a chicken wing in the air.

"How many steps ahead are you?" asked Gaylynn, raising a professionally arched eyebrow at her.

"I suffered a few frogs to find my prince. I'm the only woman at this table wearing an engagement ring," Imani replied with a superior smile. "I'll text Errol and see if he's working the night shift on Saturday. If he's working then I'm in for the play."

Gaylynn heaved a sigh. "She's got a point. I hate her, but she's got a point." Her live-in boyfriend seemed to be allergic to wedding talk.

Maida peered at Nedra over the rim of her glass as she drank. "Don't be so smug, Imani. You're not the only one who can catch a good man."

Imani blinked at her. "Say what?"

"I missed something? Spill it this minute," demanded Gaylynn.

"Not me. Nedra's keeping secrets. I had to find out on the street that she's dating Judge Jacobs' son." Maida wore a satisfied smile, even though Nedra scowled at her.

"I went to school with Trey Jacobs at St. Gerard High and Southern University. Handsome as a movie star, but he's got a rep, girl. Be careful." Imani gave a grunt.

"I've only had two dates with Carlos, not Trey. I'll tell my own business, thank you very much, Maida Grant," Nedra clipped.

"Let's get to the important news. So, Judge Jacobs has another single son?" Maida grinned and inched her chair closer to Nedra. "I can see double dating in our future, my dear and loving friend."

"Didn't you hear me say that Trey Jacobs has a rep? He's a baby daddy for one thing. Keisha Fontenot has a little boy for him. Her daddy is that lawyer who's always on television. Mr. and Mrs. Fontenot bought a huge, historic home in the Garden District. They were even on HGTV." Imani rattled off the facts as though she had a complete dossier on the Fontenot family.

"Trust Imani to know the details," Gaylynn wisecracked and helped herself to a meatball.

"Dang, people. I've only known the man since Thanksgiving. I'm not up on his family history. I don't even know if we'll do more than have a few more dates and go our separate ways."

"Nedra is right. We're all on the Twelve-Step program, not to jump into bed and start browsing bridal magazines within the first seven days of meeting a man." Maida wore a sage expression of support. "Take it slow. We need to have our own lives. We shouldn't need men, but find men who need us."

"Hear, hear," said Nedra, raising her glass. The other three women followed suit and they shared a toast.

"Fine, so by Thursday afternoon we'll firm up our plans for the play, Saturday. I'll get the tickets," Gaylynn said.

"I'll ask my neighbor to babysit when I get home. The kids love Mrs. Morrison and she enjoys having them over," Maida said.

"Errol probably knows his schedule. I'll ask him when he comes over tonight and text you," Imani replied.

"Umm, I can't. Carlos invited me to that jazz performance at the Shaw Center for the Arts, Saturday night." Nedra concentrated on loading appetizers onto her saucer.

"She met him last Thursday, had two dates, and has a third already set. Right, keep on taking it slow!" said Imani, cocking an eyebrow at the other two women.

"Dates, not sleepovers," Nedra replied.

"It sounds like he really wants to be with you. I say go for it," said Maida, winking at her.

"Yeah, he's the one making future plans. That's a good sign. I'm happy for you," Imani added.

The women switched to the other hot topic for downtown workers – city politics. Imani plunged into sharing inside gossip. As she and Gaylynn swapped stories, Maida leaned close to Nedra. "If things work out for you and Carlos, help me bump into his fine brother.

Remember your girl," she added in an undertone.

Nedra laughed out loud. "You're too much."

\*\*\*\*

On Wednesday morning, conference room 603 in the downtown municipal building filled up fast. Nedra gazed around at the volunteers, eager to get started on the Holiday Hospitality Christmas Dinner. People were arriving through the doors at either end of the room.

Constable Davidson was enjoying the social mixing before everyone got down to the planning details, but most of the work had already been done, long before the Thanksgiving dinner. All that remained was to firm up the important items. Each committee chair would report on the sponsors, the volunteers lined up for the day of the dinner, and any donated bulk food items for the menu.

Nedra happily sat back and waited for her counterpart for the Christmas event to get his ducks in a row. Rod expected all of the arrangements to be nailed down, so George Eastman, the operations coordinator, checked to make sure his sub-committee leaders had no problems to report. Rod had a good-natured face in public, as did most politicians, but he cracked his whip behind the scenes. With an eye on running for the legislature in another year, he wanted a list of good deeds to use during his campaign.

"I'm so glad to see you, guys," Rod called out as two men entered the conference room. He shook their hands and beamed.

"You think he's had enough time to feel out possible campaign donors?" George whispered over Nedra's shoulder. The tall redhead had been a basketball standout at LSU in the nineties.

She turned to him. "Trust me; he's already sealed some deals on that score. He'll be shaking hands for another hour if you let him. Just get everyone's attention and start."

"My plan, exactly. I don't want to be here until Christmas Eve," George joked. He strode over to the podium and announced that the meeting was about to start.

Nedra took a seat in a chair along the wall. She liked being an observer after her long stint as the Thanksgiving dinner operations coordinator. In true Southern style, George allowed people to gather a cup of coffee, donut or fruit, which were set out. Five minutes later, nearly everyone was seated around a long table in the center of the room.

Nedra took out her tablet and stylus to take notes. As George went over the general details, she scribbled down a few key words. More people came into the meeting, but Nedra checked her e-mails and didn't glance up. A handout containing the minutes of the previous meeting was passed around and she took one.

"Hello, pretty lady."

Nedra's head snapped around. Carlos was sitting in the once-empty chair to her left. He wore a teasing smile at her shocked reaction. She managed to recover from the thrill of hearing that mellow baritone voice. *It wouldn't do to salivate over the man in front of the whole world.*

"Well, hello," she whispered. "What are you doing here?"

"I signed on for the Christmas dinner. Seeing the smiles and happiness, and being part of making it happen feels good." Carlos leaned closer. "My buddies will be wondering about my macho image in a minute."

"Real men like to serve others," Nedra quipped and grinned back at him.

"Good you think that way. I'm going to learn how to serve you, too." Carlos winked and sat back as George started to speak again.

Nedra used the sheet of paper containing the minutes to fan her face. Carlos' sensual implication hit her body like a flamethrower and she was feeling the fire. Though she tried to focus on the drone of George's voice, her imagination fought back. Images flashed through her mind of Carlos lying naked on Egyptian cotton sheets, waiting for her with a platter of chocolate-covered strawberries. The mention of her name punched through her wonderful visualization.

"What do you think, Nedra?" George asked.

She blinked rapidly, as though trying to remember who he was and why he was there. Heads turned to gaze at her. Nedra smiled and nodded. "Sure thing."

"Which one?" George asked with a laugh.

"Sorry, uh, I was making notes. Repeat that for me again." Nedra blushed at being caught daydreaming.

She spotted Dwayne, standing next to the mayor, wearing a less-than-friendly smirk at her expense. He looked across the room and gave a slight nod in that direction. Nedra followed his gaze to find Judge Yvonne Jacobs, stone-faced and dressed in her black robe, studying her intently. Nedra cursed herself for not paying attention to who had entered the room.

"He asked if the carts worked or if we should we serve buffet style," Carlos whispered.

"Oh, right. Thanks," she replied, giving him a grateful smile. To George, she said, "Definitely use the carts again. In fact, I'll make a call and see if we can get at least a few with two levels."

"Yeah, with our crowds, buffet style wouldn't work as well. Plus we'd need separate space so the crowd wouldn't spill into the dining area," Alice Faye chimed in.

"The volunteers really enjoy the interaction of going from one table to the next. Plus doing it that way gives us a true family-style dining experience," Nedra added, getting her wind back.

"Good points, Nedra," said Rod, beaming at her. "At this late date we can't switch the location for extra space."

George nodded and smiled at Nedra. "You're on target per usual, ladies. Nedra, I'll put you down for looking to upgrade the carts. Thanks."

"No problem," she replied, adding the reminder to her tablet. She didn't look at the judge again for the rest of the meeting.

Thirty minutes later, George wrapped up the briefing and once again people took the chance to network. Judge Jacobs spoke to the Mayor, and Dwayne hovered nearby, nodding as if he was a key part of their discussion. Yet he took time to dart glances at Nedra and Carlos.

Carlos stepped in front of her, cutting off the view of Dwayne, and said, "So, you'll get to meet my mother."

"Hmm, well, she looks busy and I'm sure she has to get back to court," Nedra replied, her words tumbling out as she inched towards the nearby door.

"The judge's bite isn't fatal. I should know, since I had to live with it for nineteen years." Carlos chuckled.

"I've got to make some calls anyway. See you Saturday."

As two people opened the door, Nedra gave Carlos what she hoped was a warm smile and zipped past them to safety. Or so she thought. His long-legged stride helped him to catch up with her in the hallway.

"Nedra, hold on a minute," Carlos said, placing a guiding hand under her elbow. Nedra stopped walking. "She's really not that bad, despite what you may have heard."

"No, no, I don't listen to gossip. I mean, it's just..."

Nedra struggled for a way to not insult his mother accidently. "You know, still on the clock and lots of stuff to do."

"Tell the truth," Carlos said, one eyebrow cocked.

"Don't you think it's a little fast for a 'meet the mother' kind of thing?" Nedra replied. "We're in the early stages of... well, we really don't know what, do we?"

"True, but since we're all here and the situation happened naturally, we might as well get it over with. I already mentioned you last week and..."

"What?" Nedra yelped and then caught herself when a few heads turned. "Sorry, I'm just surprised my name came up so soon."

Carlos laughed out loud. "The expression on your face is priceless. Okay, okay, don't shoot me. We can put off the meet and greet indefinitely. Better?"

"Lord, yes. I mean, uh..." Nedra cast around for a way to dress up her reaction.

"No problem," Carlos replied, and laughed harder as he hooked an arm around her, as if he needed to support himself.

"Did I look that horrified? Please don't think I'm insulting your mother," Nedra whispered, glancing around. Then she faced him and nudged his side. "Now stop that. People are staring."

"Okay, okay. No one is paying attention. In fact, the hallway has cleared." Carlos gazed into her eyes and then at her mouth. "Saturday seems a long way off, you know?"

Nedra breathed in the scent of him; a spicy whiff with a hint of sandalwood. She swallowed hard and nodded, unable to do more. He brushed a finger along her right cheek and she shivered.

"Carlos, I didn't realize you were going to volunteer again. Holiday Hospitality events must really appeal to you."

They both turned to find Judge Jacobs standing a few feet away. Her black coffee-colored eyes shifted from her son to Nedra, and then to his arm around her. Yvonne's smile looked chilly enough to have icicles hanging from her mouth.

Carlos gave his mother a relaxed grin, lowered his arm from Nedra's shoulder and grabbed her hand. "Good morning, mother. You're right. I did have a great time on Thanksgiving Day. This is Nedra..."

"...Wallace," Judge Jacobs finished for him. "Nice to meet you. You're Rod's executive assistant." She stuck out her hand and gave Nedra a firm handshake.

"Nice to meet you as well, Judge Jacobs," Nedra replied. She stared directly back at the woman, who seemed intent on making her shiver. Instead, Nedra only became annoyed with her 'tiger mother' act. *This man is thirty-five years old, for goodness sake.*

"I'm surprised to see you at the meeting. I didn't know you were involved with the dinners or worked with Constable Davidson," Carlos said casually.

Nedra thought he seemed unaware or unaffected by his mother's intimidating aura.

Judge Jacobs' expression tightened, though she managed to maintain her frozen smile. "No, I've never had the pleasure of working with Rod on anything. The mayor and I wanted to stop in, and show our support to such a worthwhile community event."

"Exactly," Carlos replied easily, as though they were just chatting.

Nedra wondered if she imagined the undertone of dislike that seemed to color the woman's words. "The media always gives us good exposure."

"Yes," Judge Jacobs clipped. "Well, I must get back to court. I have a status hearing in ten minutes. I don't like to keep people waiting. You're welcome to have dinner with us one Sunday, Ms. Wallace."

"Thank you so much. Maybe after the holidays," Nedra replied. "What with work, volunteering and family, the next two months are going to be brutal."

"Of course. I'll be sure to remind Carlos. Goodbye, son." Judge Jacobs waited for him to respond.

"Bye, mother. Have a great day." Carlos pecked her cheek and winked at her.

Judge Jacobs smiled and gave him a slight nod, before striding away. Security officers and lawyers nodded respectfully at the imposing woman. She traded a few friendly comments with the security staff and gave restrained greetings to the lawyers. Then she disappeared around a corner that led to the elevators.

"That was fun," Nedra blurted out. "I'm sorry. I just keep..."

"Will you relax? I know the effect Mother has, or rather likes to have on people. Usually women I date can't wait to meet her. My parents stage two lavish holiday parties at Christmas and New Year's Eve. Lots of folks would love to be invited." Carlos' smile stiffened.

"I'm pretty sure I'll be busy," Nedra said quickly.

Carlos barked out a loud laugh. "You don't know the date yet. You want to stay far away from my mother. I have to say I kinda like that," he quipped.

"Will you stop?" Nedra playfully slapped him on the shoulder. Then she lowered her voice. "You do know that Rod supported your mother's opponent in her last election? And she reportedly gave help to Rod's opponent when he ran for constable. She and the mayor aren't Rod Davidson fans."

"Yes, I do know, and you pulled a nice punch in pointing out that Mother and the mayor showed for a photo opp." Carlos grinned impishly when Nedra blinked at him.

"I didn't exactly..." Nedra's voice trailed off and she avoided his gaze. "Carlos, listen, I shouldn't have gotten my back up with your mother. It's just, well, a few times she's called the office and wasn't exactly cordial. I'm afraid I ran interference for Rod when he didn't want to talk to her."

Carlos flinched. "Ouch. I'm sure she doesn't even remember that."

Nedra gave him a skeptical look. "Judge Jacobs not remember?"

"She isn't small-minded. That political stuff has nothing to do with you and me. Now smile and think of how much fun we're going to have on Saturday." He gave her a quick kiss on the forehead. "Will you meet me there or can I pick you up?"

"You can come pick me up," Nedra replied, without thinking of the rule about new dates: no trips to your home in the early stages. Not until you get to know him and confirm he's not a psycho.

"Good," he replied, giving her arm a squeeze. "Text me your address. Talk to you later tonight."

"Sure," Nedra said, and watched him stroll off with a smile plastered across her face. She turned around and bumped into someone. "Sorry."

Dwayne looked down at her. "So caught up that you're tripping over people, huh?"

"Hello, Dwayne. See you later. I have to get back to the office," Nedra said in a dry tone. She sighed inwardly when Dwayne fell in step beside her.

"So you're kicking it with the judge's favorite son?" he asked. "The mayor is running for the legislature next year; the district fourteen senate seat. I hear Rod is going to throw his name into the race."

"My boss doesn't discuss his political plans with me."

Nedra cursed the surge of people who slowed her

progress towards the elevators. Once they got there, she pressed the button hard, as if that would speed one to her.

Dwayne glanced around and lowered his voice. "Judge Jacobs and her hubby are quietly supporting the mayor's bid."

"Thanks for the update, Dwayne, but none of that has anything to do with me."

Nedra darted into the elevator with a crowd that left no room for Dwayne. She waved goodbye to him as the doors whisked shut. *Great. One more reason to keep things light with Carlos.* They could enjoy each other and never get to the 'meet the parents' stage, Nedra vowed. The last thing she wanted was a monster-in-law. Then she thought of Carlos and the way they'd talked so easily over dinner; of the way he looked at her and really saw her. Life had played a little nasty joke on her this time.

****

On Friday evening, Nedra sat in her mother's small den with her feet on the leather ottoman, which matched the rest of the furniture. Darcie Lee Wallace would have looked younger than her sixty years, but a permanent stamp of dissatisfaction marked her brow with frown lines. Still her nut brown skin had few wrinkles. She ate from a big bowl of popcorn in her lap while Gaylynn fiddled with her mother's Blu-ray player.

Nedra's older sister, Jarae, was in her mother's spare bedroom, setting up a movie and the games console to keep her own and Gaylynn's kids entertained. She had two boys, while Gaylynn had a six-year-old boy and a four-year-old girl.

Minutes later, Jarae entered the den and flopped down on the loveseat. At five feet nine and with nut brown skin like their mother, she had briefly been a model in her teens. "Damn, those kids should be tired after being at school all day and playing since they got in." She let out a deep breath.

"They're young, with energy to spare, baby. Get used to it. You got a good twenty years to go," Darcie Lee retorted. "I told y'all not to have those kids without a husband. I learned my lesson young."

"Now why did you get her started, Jarae?" Gaylynn muttered. At thirty, she already matched her mother's constantly harried look. With cinnamon skin and reddish brown hair, Gaylynn turned more than a few male heads.

"You know Mama's gonna bring that up every chance she gets. I didn't have to start her off," Jarae grunted. She was about to go on when her ten-year-old son, Noah, and his nine-year-old brother, Christian, raced in.

Darcie Lee glared at them. "What did I tell y'all about running through my house?"

"Yes, ma'am," said Christian.

"Mama, can we have some more Kool-Kid punch?" Noah waved an empty, plastic cup in the air. His little brother raised his as well.

"Y'all can only have one more cup. You'll be up all night peeing," Jarae shot back. She stood up and stomped into the kitchen, fussing as she went. Moments later, there was the pounding of feet and Jarae returned. "Kids eat and drink like bottomless pits."

"They're growing boys. Just wait until they're teenagers. Then you'll really have something to complain about," Darcie Lee replied, nodding. "Now, if you had two incomes it would be a whole lot easier."

"Look at it this way, Mama, you didn't have to chip in and pay for any weddings," Nedra joked. Then she sobered when Jarae stared daggers at her.

"I wouldn't have paid for weddings anyway. Name me one couple who stayed together, out of all my friends who paid a lot of money for fancy weddings. Name one," Darcie Lee replied.

"Make up your mind, Mama," Gaylynn shot back. "You say we should have gotten married. Then you turn around and say marriage is a waste." She tucked her legs beneath her on the sofa.

"I didn't say it was a waste. I said most of your generation doesn't have the good sense to pick the right person. Course I have to concede that you girls don't have much to choose from when it comes to men." Darcie Lee gave a sharp nod.

"You and Mr. Jesse seem to be rockin' steady. When are y'all going to get married anyway?" Jarae asked, and shot an amused look at her sisters. Jesse Franklin had been their mother's boyfriend for the last year.

"I'm talking about these young men," Darcie Lee snapped back. "My plans are none of your business."

"Well since we're talking about men and going to the altar, I don't see why we can't all be held to the same standard," Jarae replied.

"First of all, I don't have young kids to support, so I'm in no hurry. I'm not going to have any more babies either. I don't care what these other women are doing, having babies in their fifties and sixties. That's slap crazy." Darcie Lee shook her head. "Jesse and I have raised our children. Now we can relax and take things slow."

"I'm just checking. We could start picking out your wedding dress and deciding on colors for the bridesmaids." Jarae pressed her lips together to keep from laughing, and cut another glance at Gaylynn and Nedra.

"At least I have a decent man with a job and who

treats me with respect," Darcie Lee replied and raised an eyebrow at her.

"Yeah, yeah," Jarae muttered.

Jarae's last boyfriend had turned out to be a true disaster. He called himself a music producer. What he really did was sit around, pretending to be a big shot and living off Jarae. After dating for six months, she had allowed him to move in with her while his condo was being "renovated". The temporary arrangement turned permanent. Later, Jarae learned that he'd been living with another woman who had thrown him out. He was a habitual moocher, moving from one gravy train to the next.

Nedra nudged Gaylynn secretly. "Let's change the subject fast."

Her sister nodded. "Well, at least Nedra has a hot prospect; a judge's son."

"No, you didn't," said Nedra through clenched teeth. She squinted at Gaylynn, who shrugged an apology and mouthed, "Sorry".

"Say what?" Jarae stared at Nedra. Resentment simmered in her light brown eyes. "Excuse us, Ms. Big Time Connections."

Darcie Lee put aside the bowl of popcorn. "What judge and what's the man's name?"

"We've just been on a couple of dates. It's no big deal," Nedra replied, jabbing her elbow into Gaylynn's side.

"Ouch! You didn't say it was a secret." Gaylynn inched to the other end of the loveseat and out of her sister's reach.

"Nedra, why so hush hush? Spill the details," said Jarae, seeming to enjoy her discomfort.

"We just met. We might not even see each other for long." Nedra picked up the remote and turned on the movie.

"Stop," Darcie Lee said and pointed a finger at her. "I asked you a question Nedra Denise."

"His name is Carlos Jacobs and…"

"Yvonne Jacobs' son? Humph, that's going to be interesting when you meet her. She can't stand your boss," Darcie Lee said.

"And she's not known for being warm and cuddly either," Gaylynn added. "My friend, Shae, worked in her law firm before she got elected. She said the woman is mean as hell when she's in a bad mood, and she's in a bad mood ninety percent of the time." She laughed and slapped the loveseat cushion.

"I've already met her, but only because we ran into each other at a meeting the other day. It went just fine," Nedra said. No need to mention that keeping the time brief had helped. "But that doesn't matter because, like I said, we've only had a few dates."

"You just met when?" Darcie Lee probed.

"Thanksgiving Day," Nedra replied and fidgeted with the remote.

"At the Holiday Hospitality dinner. He volunteered," Gaylynn explained. She broke off when Nedra glared at her again.

"So you just met him a little over a week ago and you've had 'a few dates' already? No wonder Gaylynn mentioned him. Hmm." Darcie Lee lapsed into thoughtful silence.

"Okay, let me get something straight right now." Nedra stood to emphasize her point. "I hardly know the guy, okay? No, I'm not bringing him here to meet everyone. So don't make this a big deal. Now let's watch the movie." She sat down again.

"I've got two daughters who had kids too fast, and another one with a ticking biological clock who can't seem to make up her mind."

Nedra gazed at Darcie Lee steadily. "Drop. It.

Mama."

Her mother held up both hands. "Okay, okay. I'm just saying, Nedra."

"I'm happy. I have an exciting job, great friends and an apartment I love." Nedra took in a deep breath and then let it out. "Let's try to have a fun evening watching this murder mystery."

Darcie Lee picked up the now half-empty bowl of popcorn. "Fine, I'll get more popcorn and soft drinks."

"I'll go check on the kids," Gaylynn said and shot from her seat before anyone could object.

Jarae smirked. "Another entertaining night with the Wallace girls."

"Oh shut it, Jarae," Nedra tossed back.

## Chapter 4

Saturday evening had turned into a magical experience for Nedra. Carlos picked her up a half hour before the jazz performance. The band dazzled the crowd with smooth performances of the standards and a few modern compositions of their own.

After the concert ended, she walked with Carlos a few blocks away to a steak restaurant. Don's Steak and Seafood took up the fourth floor of a restored nineteen-thirties building. They had a view of the Mississippi River and the long bridge connecting Baton Rouge to the small town of Port Allen. Lights along the bridge and other buildings, including two riverboat casinos, twinkled against the deep blue night sky.

Nedra sighed as she gazed out through the floor-to-ceiling windows. "This is beautiful," she said, "and the food here is really good. Nice choice."

"I'm glad you enjoyed your steak," replied Carlos, taking a sip of his red wine.

"Oh yes. This sweet potato bread pudding should be against the law. I'm taking the rest of it home. I can't eat that huge serving. Why did you talk me into getting my own instead of us sharing?" Nedra shook a finger at him.

"Because this way we'll have some to enjoy with coffee later," Carlos said smoothly and smiled at her.

"Well, I sure can't fit any more food in here," Nedra answered, patting her mid-section.

"I have a suggestion. The evening isn't too cold. In fact the weather is quite pleasant. Let's work off dinner with a stroll."

"You know I work down here, yet I rarely do anything but go to the office and go home. I haven't even seen the parks and walking paths on top of the levee." Nedra glanced out of the window.

"Then let's go." Carlos signaled to their waiter.

A few minutes later they were outside. After a quick detour to put their doggie bags of food in his car, Nedra and Carlos headed towards the riverside pedestrian park. Arms linked, they enjoyed the crisp night air and the riverfront for another thirty minutes. They talked about a range of subjects, including the upcoming college football season. Carlos took great delight in learning that Nedra also enjoyed basketball. Soon they were making plans for a trip to New Orleans to see a game. Forty-five minutes later, they were back at the parking garage.

They got into the Acura, but Carlos paused after putting his key in the ignition. "Now we can enjoy that rich bread pudding without feeling guilty," he said.

"Here, right now?" Nedra laughed. "That walk definitely stirred up your appetite."

"No, girl, back at my place where it's warmer and there's cable." Carlos started the car and backed out of the parking space.

"Oh." Nedra started running through different ways to avoid going to his place.

"I can finally break in that fancy coffee maker that my mother gave me when I bought my townhouse. I've had that thing for two years, but used it once when she came over." Carlos laughed. "Good thing she hasn't thought to ask about it again."

Nedra stared out the windshield straight ahead. "Listen, about going to your house..."

"If you're not comfortable with going to my townhouse, we can go to your place. I'll stop and get you some pepper spray. You can zap me if I get out of hand." Carlos stopped the car and put it in park again. "I don't have an agenda, Nedra. Honest."

"Oh, I wasn't thinking you did. Well, maybe a little. I just don't want us to get our wires crossed, and you think that... I don't want to mislead you to think…"

"No, I don't think you're willing to jump into sex quickly with any guy that buys you a steak dinner." Carlos placed a hand over one of hers. "This might come off like a line, but it's true. I feel something special for you, Nedra. We'll take whatever time is needed to get to the next level and when we're both comfortable. Okay?"

Nedra gazed into his eyes and saw sincerity. Carlos brushed a thumb against her cheek. Then he leaned over and gently kissed her lips. No tongue-down-her-throat kind of kiss, but a caress that lasted a few moments before he sat back.

"Okay," Nedra replied softly.

"Great. Now we'll call it a night so you can rest up and we can come back to the downtown square to listen to the band tomorrow afternoon." He shifted to drive again.

"But I have a fancy coffee maker, too," she said quietly. "No need in us being wasteful and making coffee in two places."

Carlos grinned at her. "I'm big on being green."

Twenty minutes later, they arrived at Nedra's condo, off Bluebonnet Avenue. She didn't feel any apprehension as they entered her second floor, two-bedroom flat. They took off their jackets and Nedra placed the bags of leftover steak and extra bread, which the waiter had given them, in her fridge. Then she gave Carlos a short tour. Returning to the kitchen, she put the coffee on to brew. With the R&B music channel playing on the television, they sat in the living room, where they talked and traded jokes. The smell of coffee floated in from the kitchen.

"I think it's ready," Nedra said, standing.

"That bread pudding is calling to me," he said. "Carlos, we're meant for each other. Come for me, my love."

Nedra giggled. "Yeah, right. Just admit you're

greedy when it comes to sugar. I wonder how you keep so fit."

"Hmm, so you like my look. Good to know." Carlos struck a pose and then pretended to walk like a male model. "I'm going to keep working out, so I can hold on to my good thing."

"You're so crazy," Nedra replied and giggled even harder. "You know, I thought you'd be all serious and… I don't know."

"Stuck up? Arrogant?" Carlos stopped clowning around and followed her into the kitchen.

Nedra faced him. "Well, maybe. I'm glad you're not."

"Speaking of looking good…" Carlos took both of her hands in his. "I'm happy I ended up at the Holiday Hospitality dinner. Meeting you is something I'm definitely thankful for."

"I glad we met, too," she said. Her heart melted at the look in his beautiful, brown eyes.

"I've been dating for the past eight months, since I broke up with someone. We have a five-year-old daughter. Chanté wanted a baby, but I didn't. We tried to make it work, but we just weren't good together. We argue sometimes because Chanté moved to Houston. She doesn't always make it easy for me to see my daughter." Carlos frowned.

"What's your little girl's name?" Nedra asked, feeling a pang.

"Carly. We stuck with the 'C' theme," Carlos quipped.

"That's a pretty name, " she replied. "I'm guessing she's a daddy's girl."

"All the way," he said. "She'll be here for Christmas since she spent Thanksgiving with her mother's family this year. That's it. No serious drama." Carlos gazed at Nedra as though looking for a sign.

"Thanks for telling me."

Every moment they spent together brought them closer; connected in a real way. This time Nedra kissed him. She pulled Carlos against her body and wrapped both of her arms around him. Their second kiss lasted longer, much longer. When they broke apart, he let out a slow breath.

"We better have dessert and coffee before you have to slap my face." He let go of Nedra and put a hand on his chest. "Whew."

"I could be making a mistake about you, but I'm going to break my first date rule." Nedra pulled him to her again. Guiding his hands to her hips, she gave him another passionate kiss. When she stopped, both of them were breathing hard.

"This isn't our first date," Carlos said, resting his forehead against hers.

"Technically, it's our first full date." Nedra rubbed her lips against his neck, savoring the sensation. She gasped when he grew harder.

"Are you sure you should break that rule? I'm willing to wait, even if it means spending a night of torture, home alone in my bed." Carlos let out a soft moan as Nedra's fingers lightly brushed his erection beneath the fabric of his slacks.

"You want me to break that rule. Say it," she whispered and nibbled on his right ear lobe.

"Yes! Oh hell, yes." Carlos rested his forehead against hers and sighed.

Without speaking, Nedra took his hand and led him into her bedroom. They undressed in front of each other and savored the process as each item of clothing fell onto the carpet. Nedra's practical side tried to gain her attention, but the vow she'd taken with her friends fell on deaf ears.

When Carlos wrapped her in a loving embrace, skin

against skin, Nedra felt cherished, not cheap. Each kiss and caress reinforced her first instinct after looking into his eyes on Thanksgiving Day. The charged heat between them was more than a quick sexual itch. When he touched her intimately and whispered with tenderness, all of her doubts and reservations went up in smoke. The hours of love, joy and happiness left them both breathless, speechless and exhausted.

## Chapter 5

Sunday went by much too fast, thought Nedra on Monday morning. She sat at her desk, enjoying a rich, chocolate mocha latte in her favorite mug. The waiting stack of papers did not speak to her at all. Fortunately, the administrative assistant she supervised was doing the heavy lifting of answering the phones and her boss would not be in until after lunch, so Nedra had the luxury of replaying her wonderful weekend over and over again. Finally, she shook off her dream state and began working, though not at her usual pace.

When her friend, Imani, came into the office, Nedra grinned at her. "Happy Monday morning," she said. "I'm loving this cold weather we're having. It's just right for the holiday season."

"Morning," Imani replied, sitting down in the chair facing Nedra's desk. She frowned. "Mondays suck like sewer water."

"So you didn't have a good weekend?" Nedra laughed when her friend screwed up her face into a macabre expression. "Errol had to work again?"

"He's working overtime because he'll have Christmas off. At least that's what he says," Imani muttered. Her brows pulled together. "I can't even get him on his cell phone sometimes."

Nedra shook her head. "The man is at work, Imani. He can't be chatting with you. You're complaining because the man has a great job and is hard working? He's making money, which means a nice Christmas present for, guess who?"

Imani's expression brightened. "I like your logic, so what about you?"

"Me?" Nedra cleared her throat and moved some papers around on her desk.

"Hello, hello, hello. How's everybody?" Maida asked as she slid into the other chair in Nedra's office. "Thank God for Mondays."

"What?" Imani blinked at her.

"You obviously don't have kids, girl. Saturday, Chalice had a soccer game. Jon had a football game. His daddy took him, but then decided I'd have to pick him up. Thankfully, Mama agreed to help me out and the kids stayed with her, so I could keep my hair appointment. And I managed to talk her into babysitting, so I could go to the play with Imani," Maida said.

"It wasn't bad at all," Imani put in.

"How would you know? You kept checking your phone for text messages," Maida retorted.

"Oh, shut up," Imani mumbled.

"Uh-huh," Maida replied, giving her a side eye, and then resumed her narrative. "Sunday, I took them to their grandmother's church across town. Jonathan insisted because his mother wanted to see them, so I hauled them across the river to New Roads. Did their daddy bring them back? No, that would have been considerate, so I had to drive back and pick the kids up. Sunday night we got ready for the week." Maida eyed Nedra's mug.

"Yes, I have a pot of mocha chocolate coffee because I figured you guys might want some." Nedra nodded in the direction of the office kitchenette. They typically met up for a Monday morning coffee break.

"Bless you," said Maida and left.

"Me, too," said Imani and followed her out.

The two women soon returned, carrying large paper cups with steam rising. Both got settled again. They commiserated about the agony of work and the unreasonableness of bosses. Then talk turned back to the weekend.

"So, make me feel better. At least I can live vicariously by listening to you two describe fun weekend activities." Maida blew on her coffee and took a sip.

"Sorry, I can't help," Imani retorted. Then she eyed Nedra over her fashionable eyeglasses. "But Nedra was just about to tell me about her weekend with the new man."

"Oo-wee. Tell it, girl. Tell it all." Maida wiggled her eyebrows and nodded.

"Yes, Nedra, you had a date Saturday night, as I recall." Imani sat back and crossed her long legs. "We're listening."

"We had a nice time," Nedra replied mildly, and stopped when the young woman she supervised entered. She took several pieces of sorted mail. When the assistant was gone, Nedra shrugged. "So, did Jon and Chalice win their games?"

"His team lost, Chalice's team won. Now back to your night with Carlos Jacobs," Maida instructed.

"Yeah, you're the one playing games," Imani said. "Tell us about the jazz concert."

"And dinner after," Maida added, with a glance at Imani.

"That's right. And did you serve up some juicy dessert to the man?" Imani added.

"We're not in middle school," Nedra retorted and waved a hand. "The concert was great. They even mixed in some rap with the jazz. The older folks seemed a bit puzzled, but most of the audience was our generation. We did our chair dance performances." Nedra did a few moves and grinned at the memory.

"So y'all jammed at the concert . Then you had dinner, and..." Imani gestured for Nedra to go on.

"Dinner downtown was great. Then we went for a walk along the levee." Nedra looked out of the window of her fourth-floor office. "You know, the Downtown Development initiative has really done wonders with the walking path. Baton Rouge is pretty at night."

"Umm, sounds magical. And then he took you home?" Maida sat forward in her chair and put her cup down.

Nedra snapped out of her reverie to find her friends staring at her intently. "Right. So, like I said, we had a nice time."

"Uh-huh." Imani looked at Maida.

"Yeah, they had a nice evening. Did it end with him leaving you on your doorstep?" Maida lifted one eyebrow.

"He came in for coffee and sweet potato bread pudding. They give you huge portions of the stuff, but it's so delicious. Have y'all tried it?" Nedra picked up her mug and drank deeply.

"Errol keeps promising to take me to Don's downtown, but he's always working." Imani frowned for a few seconds and then looked at Nedra again. "So you let him into your apartment?"

"How long was he there?" Maida seemed to hold her breath.

Nedra let a few seconds of suspenseful silence stretch. She sighed. "Okay, Carlos stayed for hours."

"You broke the rule," Imani whispered, her eyes wide. She looked at Maida. "She broke the rule, girl."

"We're grown women," Nedra snapped. "We make our own rules if it feels right. At some point I have to trust my own judgment again. So, I made a few mistakes. That doesn't mean I can't tell a bum from a gem."

Maida looked at Imani and then back at Nedra. "If you say so. I've heard that Carlos has been a major player on the dating scene for a while. In fact, they say the reason he broke up with his baby's mother is because she caught him cheating. Word is he went to a friend's wedding in Atlanta one weekend and..."

"Are you seriously going to spread third-hand gossip

from something that allegedly happened hundreds of miles away?" Nedra put down her mug and crossed her arms.

"Duh, hell, yeah! I'm tryin' ta help you." Maida looked at Imani, who nodded in agreement.

"How long ago was this supposed incident?" Nedra broke in before Maida could continue.

"Let's see, the baby was six months old, so that's been..."

"Quite a long time ago, since his daughter is five now," Nedra said.

Imani chewed her lip for a few seconds. "Okay, Maida, but let's tell it all. I also heard that his baby's mama hooked up with an old boyfriend at a high-school reunion."

"Let's be in solidarity with our sister. Maybe she was still in pain after what Carlos did and needed a little tenderness from a man who understood her." Maida looked at her friend.

"Nah, I heard some other stuff about her. They say there was plenty of drama between them."

"Okay, just stop." Nedra held up one palm as though she was a school crossing guard. "Do I need to remind you of our own dramatic stories from back in the day? Do you really want me to take it there?"

"Well, everybody had missteps and mistakes." Maida shrugged. "Okay, you make a good point."

"Exactly. What Carlos did then is in the past. I sure can't judge him." Nedra gave a shudder at the thought of some of her relationship failures.

"So you're having a good time, taking it light and easy?" Maida blinked at Nedra.

"Or is he the one?" Imani finished.

Nedra stared into her mug for a few minutes as though seeking the answer in the dark, still hot liquid. "Light and easy, definitely. I'm not on some safari, hunting down Mr. Right."

"Liar," Maida wisecracked. "Every single woman I know is looking for Mr. Good Thing, who will stick around."

"And how is that desperate woman thing working out for most of us?" Nedra countered. When her friends didn't answer, she nodded. "Exactly. Look, I don't want to be alone, but most of all I don't want to grab at someone just so I won't be alone. I need someone who honestly values me as a person; as a human being with ideas, goals and dreams."

"I'd settle for honesty, period. Men who lie and conceal the whole story just make me so damn mad," Imani replied, slapping the arm of her chair.

"You need to calm the hell down, girl. Trying to control Errol even when y'all are apart may drive him away. Besides, if he's going to cheat, playing detective won't stop him. Believe me; a determined cheater has his game tight." Maida gave a snort. "Ask me how I know."

"Have you heard something about him?" Imani blurted out and stared at Maida intently. You have?"

"No, there is no word on the street about Errol," Maida replied firmly. "I'm just telling you that stalking the man won't work if he's into someone else."

"Thanks for the encouraging words." Imani's frown deepened and she chewed on her fingernails.

"Just talk to Errol, Imani. Be direct, no games," Nedra said. "And stop gnawing on those fake nails before you get some kind of chemical poisoning."

Imani snatched her hand away from her mouth. "You're right. I'm going to confront him tonight. No more of this crap about him being too tired to talk."

"No, I think you just tell him you feel like y'all are getting distant and try to get him to open up about how he feels." Nedra sipped from her mug.

"When did you become a couples' therapist?" asked Maida, wearing a crooked grin.

"Umm, I read that in an article on relationships, written by an expert. Makes a lot of sense, too," Nedra added.

"I'll get him to 'fess up," Imani said and stood.

"No, Imani, I didn't say..." Nedra glanced at Maida.

"My boss has a meeting in an hour, and naturally I have to get her some talking points. Thanks for the great advice." Imani waved goodbye and walked out, wearing a preoccupied expression.

"Oh, Lord, poor Errol. Imani is making the same mistake; smothering the guy and trying to control him, and he seems so nice," Nedra said and sighed.

"The sad part is he really seems to care for her. She's so consumed with watching his every move and trying to play games that she's missing that part." Maida shook her head.

"I tried to talk to her about it. You see how far I've gotten," Nedra replied.

"So did I. Well, we gave it a shot. Now back to you." Maida pointed a forefinger at Nedra.

"Carlos is wonderful, really down to earth. I like that he's been open about his baby mama drama. We did have a wonderful night together, Saturday." Nedra sighed and leaned back in her chair.

"Hmm, I see, and what about his mother?" Maida raised an eyebrow.

"She wasn't there," Nedra wisecracked and laughed. "That would have put a huge strain on the good times, for sure."

"Speaking of women who like control, Judge Jacobs supposedly rules her family with an iron fist. Grown children or not, I hear she's a big-time meddler. Look up 'control freak' in the dictionary and they've got her photo next to the definition." Maida nodded.

"You're as bad as Dwayne Grover. How do you collect all this 'he says, she says' news anyway?" Nedra looked at her friend in wonder.

"Working in the clerk of courts office puts me in the hub of all kinds of activity. Lawyers come in to file papers. Folks come in to pay fines or court costs. They all like to unburden themselves." Maida winked at Nedra mischievously.

"In other words, you're a committed gossip. Like I said, just like Dwayne." Nedra rolled her eyes.

"Mr. Happy Hands," her friend quipped.

"You got that right, but one day he's going to grope the wrong one." Nedra grimaced with distaste.

"Nope," said Maida, waving a hand. "He's slimy, but Dwayne isn't stupid. He picks women who want male attention. His wife likes her social position and the money, so she's not squawking."

"You know his wife?" Nedra blinked, amazed at the depth of her knowledge.

"Nope, but I've met people who have known her family for years. They're wannabes." Maida lifted her nose in the air.

"Oh yeah, eager to be part of the whole black upper-class nonsense," Nedra said.

"Right. Oh, and here's something you should know: Judge Jacobs and the mayor despise your boss. It goes back to before she ran for office. I hear she's still pissed that Rod and his social circle snubbed the Jacobs family back in the day. And, of course, our esteemed mayor is so proud of his 'blue-collar' roots."

Nedra felt a stab of unease in her mid-section. "Their feud has nothing to do with me."

"Judge Jacobs may see you as part of the enemy camp, girlfriend, and she's known for holding grudges. What's going to happen when Rod and his crew run for office? You know the Judge and her posse are going to oppose him."

"Girl, please. The election is in November of next year," Nedra protested.

Maida shook her head. "The behind-the-scenes campaign started this year. By February, Rod and the mayor will ramp up politicking. You'll be in a tight spot if Carlos has to tow his mama's party line."

"Carlos is not into politics. Even he was, his mother wouldn't dictate to him. He's a grown man. But more than that, we might not be dating past Christmas for all I know." Nedra's body thrummed at the memory of being in his arms. Nothing about what they shared felt temporary.

Maida stood, leaned across the desk, and snapped her fingers inches away from Nedra's nose. "Yoo-hoo! Wake up. You fell into a mesmerizing daze just thinking about Saturday night. From the look on your face, I'd say you better start thinking of ways you can co-exist with Judge Monster Mama. You ain't planning on leaving that fine man behind. Uh-uh."

Nedra tried to laugh off her suggestion. "Trust me, we're not even near the stage where we try to figure out family issues. For now it's just the two of us. I'm going to keep it that way for a good while; months at least."

"Okay. You just keep saying that to yourself," said Maida, glancing at her smartphone. "Dang, better get back to the office. Let's have lunch?"

"Sorry, but I have a meeting. I don't know when we'll finish up. Tomorrow is better for me. We'll call Imani in the morning and see if she can make it." Nedra glanced at a file on her desk with sticky notes on the outside.

Maida's eyes lit up with interest. "Great idea. We can get the story on how her 'talk' with Errol turns out."

"I wasn't thinking of that," replied Nedra, giving her a scolding expression. "If she wants to tell us, it's fine. If not then that's okay, too.

"We both know Imani will spill it." Maida touched the screen of her smartphone. "I'm going to make sure my calendar is free for lunch. Talk to you later."

Nedra shook her head at Maida. "You're too much. Goodbye girl."

For the rest of the day, as she took calls for her boss and sat next to him in meetings, Nedra thought about politics. Maybe she should take her own advice and bring up the subject with Carlos. At two o'clock that afternoon, sat at her desk eating a late lunch, Nedra decided that Maida was dead wrong on all counts. She pushed aside any thoughts of her personal and professional lives becoming complicated.

****

A few blocks away, Carlos sat across a table from his mother in her spacious office. They shared some take-out Greek food that he'd picked up for their lunch together. The scent of roasted lamb, garlic and onions filled the room as though they were in the downtown restaurant where the food had been prepared. Carlos tried to steer the conversation to his mother's day in the courtroom.

"I don't understand why you're hiding the Wallace woman," said Yvonne as she took out two bottles of green tea from a compact refrigerator in the corner of the room.

"We're not hiding," Carlos replied for the second time. He sighed deeply for the third time. The effort to keep his temper would most likely give him heartburn soon, if he didn't lose his appetite altogether.

Yvonne found a pack of napkins. She poured some tea into two tall, styrofoam cups and placed them on the table. "Here you go. You always want extra napkins. I hope you have extra cucumber sauce – you love that on your gyros more than I do. Well, it sure looks like you're hiding this relationship to me. Even your father is wondering about it."

Carlos tried not to get annoyed at his mother's fussing and sighed yet again. "Nedra and I are in the 'getting to know each other' process. We may not even be dating after the holidays."

"You're already having problems, huh? Well, I'm not at all surprised. She's from one of those old Baton Rouge families. Her mother lives in Thompson Heights. They don't have as much money as us, but they still think they're superior." Yvonne sniffed and went back to putting cucumber sauce on her gryos.

Carlos had no desire to stoke the smoldering fires of his mother's resentment of Baton Rouge and old, black moneyed families. He carefully picked at the food before him and warily considered his next words. "Nedra and I aren't having any problems. She's sweet and caring, and we haven't talked about her family history. She's not like that," he replied in a calm tone with no hint of defensiveness. His mother was trying to push his buttons.

"Humph," Yvonne replied, and ate some more of her lunch in silence. After a few minutes, she sipped her tea and patted her lips with a napkin. "You know she's going to be campaigning for that boss of hers."

"We haven't discussed politics, so I don't think it matters." Carlos continued to concentrate on his food.

"It will come up, Carlos. I'm supporting Mayor Bates in the state senatorial race, as you well know," his mother replied, her tone insistent. She had attended law school with Kevin Bates and they shared a deep dislike for Constable Davidson.

Carlos gave up pretending that he wanted to eat.

"That is months in the future, and it won't be a topic of conversation between Nedra and I. Look, where Nedra's mother lives and Rod Davidson's political ambitions have nothing to do with us. Please don't try to insert yourself into my love life again. I'll give you the 'I'm a grown man' speech if necessary."

"Excuse me. I was trying to have a reasonable discussion with you. I'm not getting into your personal business." Yvonne sipped some more tea and cleared her throat. "You don't have to throw a hissy fit about your latest fling. I'm sure there will be many others, as you said."

"I didn't say anything about..." Carlos stopped, counted to five and closed the top of the plastic box containing his lunch. "Nedra is not some fling. She's not a woman I plan to throw away later."

"So this is serious?" Yvonne latched onto his words, raising both eyebrows. "Well, well, well."

"I also didn't mean to imply that we're making wedding plans. We like each other and we're dating; that's it. She's smart, funny and has good common sense. I can talk to her. She's..." Carlos tried to put into words how Nedra made him feel. "She's not looking to get something out of me."

Yvonne gazed at him. "I see."

He held up his hands, palms out. "Nothing complicated, Mother. We're having fun, getting closer to see if... where we're going. Which could mean going our separate ways," Carlos added quickly.

Yvonne tilted her head to one side. "Let me say one last thing and then I'll drop the subject."

Carlos didn't believe her, but couldn't be bothered to argue. "Fine," he replied.

"Rod Davidson is a two-fisted campaigner. Don't let that jolly, teddy bear facade fool you. He'll look for any scrap of mud to throw at Kevin. If he gets wind of that little incident and the fact that the mayor helped us out..." Her voice trailed off.

Carlos did not return her gaze. "I wasn't charged with a felony. The district attorney and police didn't break any laws or rules."

"No one will care; not if they hear that you got caught up in an investigation of drug dealers," Yvonne argued. "Thank God they had no proof that you helped conceal cocaine and marijuana in those SUVs you detailed. Why in the world you opened a business in the hood..."

"Pop wanted me to stand on my own, so he didn't loan me the money for a better location. Besides, not all of my customers turned out to be drug dealers. There are a lot of good people in Easy Town," added Carlos referred to the high crime area of the city.

"So, Ms. Wallace knows you were doing the last few hours of your community service at the Thanksgiving dinner?" Yvonne asked mildly.

Carlos swallowed past the lump in his throat. "No. I mean not yet."

His mother leaned forward. "Not ever, Carlos. This isn't just about you. I have an election, too."

Silence stretched several beats before he sighed and muttered, "Fine."

## Chapter 6

Nedra looked at the lights downtown with a wide grin, feeling like a little girl again. The second weekend in December brought on the first city-sponsored celebration. A band played on the square in front of city hall.

After a short speech, Mayor Bates and several other officials flipped the switches to light a huge Christmas tree. Holiday lights strung up in the huge old trees graced the boulevard and hung from street lamps. Sparkling LED bulbs in the shape of stars dangled from street signs as well. A cheer went up and the local band went back to playing jazzy holiday tunes.

"You're really into Christmas lights, I see," said Carlos, squeezing Nedra's hand as he spoke into her ear.

"Since the first time I saw them. My daddy would put up our tree the Saturday after Thanksgiving. We had treats and sang songs. Then he'd let us turn on the lights." Nedra blinked at the happy memory of a warm, loving man. "Those were good times."

Carlos pulled her closer to him. "Sounds like a great guy, your daddy."

"He was," Nedra replied and cleared her throat. She pushed against the heartache that came from knowing she wouldn't see him again.

"So when do we put up your tree?" Carlos asked.

"I don't usually bother, not since... Besides, it's just me. What's the point?" Nedra shrugged.

"Hey, I'm sorry for bringing up a sad subject." Carlos squeezed her hand again.

"No, no," she replied. She swiped at her eyes quickly and smiled at him. "I should be apologizing for ruining our fun night."

"It's nowhere near ruined. Let's get some hot

chocolate and then we can shake our booties to some swamp rock Christmas tunes." Carlos tugged her arm towards one of several food vendors.

Nedra burst out laughing. "Did you just say we'd shake our booties? Seriously, Carlos?"

"I'm sure your father would approve. He was a party, 'let the good times roll' kinda guy. Am I right?" asked Carlos, grinning as he walked backwards in front of Nedra.

She grinned back at him. "You're right. Daddy loved to 'shake his groove thang', as he used to say. He loved all those old-school R&B Christmas tunes, and he and mama were both pretty good dancers."

"Then we have to continue the family tradition." Carlos did a few dance steps and then spun in a complete circle as the band played a version of *Frosty the Snowman*.

"I doubt the guy who wrote that song would recognize it," Nedra said with a laugh. "Now let's warm up with some hot chocolate."

"Okay, but don't think you're not going to shake it before this night is over," he tossed back and pointed a finger at her.

Nedra looped her arm through his. "Maybe."

They continued walking towards the food stand, and got into a light-hearted debate over whether Nedra would loosen up and dance with him, along with the crowd. She was once again wrapped in the pleasure of being with Carlos, and the cheerful mood of everyone at the lighting ceremony. They finally got two cups of hot chocolate with marshmallows floating on top.

Carlos took the lead, and guided Nedra on a stroll around the lighted square and down Third Street. Restaurants were decorated and shops were crowded with people buying gifts. Children giggled and raced from one window display to the next, with adults in tow.

Nedra sighed at the swell of warmth inside of her, which didn't come from the creamy, warm liquid she was drinking.

"This is the way the holidays should feel," Carlos said, as though he could read her thoughts.

"I know." Nedra watched young children enjoying the sights and sounds. "My parents did everything they could to make Christmas magical for us as kids. That's what I miss most about not being part of a family; the holidays."

"My memories aren't all warm and fuzzy," Carlos said, but his laughter sounded forced. "Let's find a table away from the crowd."

"Oh, okay," replied Nedra, worried that he might think she was dropping hints about where their relationship should go.

As they walked, Carlos talked about everything but the holiday season. They had to go around the corner near the Shaw Arts Center, past a fountain sparkling with multicolored lights and down another half block. Carlos managed to snag a small table outside, just as a couple got up to go.

"So how is work?" Nedra asked.

"Exhausting, but I'm not complaining. At least we've got customers. A lot of folks are driving into town to spend time with family, which means their cars get dirty," replied Carlos. He appeared to relax with the change of subject and grinned at her. "*CJ's Detailing* to the rescue."

"That's great. Where is your shop?" Nedra watched his expression tighten slightly.

"Um, it's on the corner of Acadian and North Street, Easy Town. A lot of folks said I was crazy to open my shop in 'Da Hood', but there are good people who live there," Carlos said with a trace of defensiveness in his voice.

Nedra nodded. "I don't believe in calling neighborhoods 'ghettos' or even bad. It's the criminals who spoil some areas of town. Easy Town and The Bottom were great places back in the day. Previous generations of blue-collar, decent folks raised families there. You're part of the solution. You provide jobs and hope."

"Jobs maybe, but I don't know about hope." Carlos held up his big, insulated cup and drank more hot chocolate. He cleared his throat.

"No, you do," said Nedra. "Many businesses have fled the inner-city areas. A lot of folks have to drive several miles to a grocery store. I think Councilwoman Terrebonne is right. Easy Town needs something more than liquor stores, bars and payday loan shops."

"Wow, you really laid out the issues. Sounds like you could be running for office in the future." Carlos grinned when Nedra let out a yelp.

She gave a melodramatic shudder. "Don't even joke about me becoming a politician. I don't have the patience or the ability to, um, creatively spin facts. No way."

"Seems a shame, since you're so passionate about the issues," replied Carlos, gazing at Nedra with mischief in his eyes.

She shook her head. "I've seen politics from the inside. No thanks. Rod is a diplomat. Me? I'd blurt out some unpleasant truth and be in trouble all the time. I'm happy hanging with regular, honest folks like you." She brushed a hand along his cheek.

"I can't claim sainthood by any stretch," Carlos said quickly.

"Nobody can. I appreciate how... real you are with me. No games or slick talk. Believe me, that's a nice change." Nedra sighed. "Listen, if I made you uncomfortable earlier talking about family, I apologize. I wasn't trying to steer the conversation toward you and I getting serious."

"Nedra, I didn't think…"

"You're so sweet, Carlos. I'm enjoying what we have right now. Don't worry. I won't give you the 'we need to talk' speech." She leaned against him and breathed in the spicy scent he wore.

"Remember I started the discussion," Carlos replied. "Besides, Christmas is about love, joy and giving. Don't hold back on telling me how to feel; about anything." He put an arm around her shoulders.

"You see? Honesty. That means a lot to me." Nedra kissed his cheek and then rubbed the slight lipstick smudge from his skin.

Carlos gazed ahead into the distance. "Yeah."

"Hey, back to love and joy," Nedra said, nudging him to shake off the serious mood he had lapsed into. "When will your little girl come to visit?"

"December twenty-second," he answered. His thoughtful expression relaxed into a smile. "Carly is excited, too. She's called me at least six times to firm up our plans. We go to the movies, see the downtown lights here, and then we pick a city to drive to and we have dinner out at least once."

Nedra smiled. "Sounds like daddy is just as excited."

"She usually stays through New Year's Day. Even though her mother will drive down to visit her family, Carly will be with me." Carlos sighed. "She's growing up so fast."

. "At five? You have a few more years of breathing space before she hits the teen years. At her age she still idolizes her old man." Nedra giggled at his pained expression

"Ouch." Carlos nudged Nedra. "Please don't use the 'old man' phrase. I'm sure I'll be getting that one from her soon enough. Besides she's already asking for her own cell phone and tablet computer. She's talking like a tween right now."

"Girls mature faster than boys." Nedra sipped the last of her hot chocolate, which was now barely warm.

"Dang, you're full of good news for 'the old man', aren't you?" Carlos pulled a hand over his face in mock despair.

"Okay, relax," she said with a laugh. "You've got time to prepare. You'll have to keep up with trends so you'll know what to watch out for."

"You sound like an expert. I bet you'd make a terrific mother, by the way." He winked at her.

Nedra blinked hard at his words and choked up, but tried to keep her tone light. She didn't want to sound like one of those 'my biological clock is ticking' females. Men ran away screaming from those single ladies.

"Thank you," she said quietly and cleared her throat. "Okay, what do we do next?"

"Let's see." Carlos pulled out his smartphone and touched the screen. "Here is the schedule of events. We can go through the Joyeux Noel Tunnel of Lights on the grounds of the Old State Capital. Or we can go to the old Governor's Mansion and see how it would have been decorated back in the 1930s. They'll have carolers in period dress in another half hour once the band stops blasting jams. Or..."

Nedra peered at his phone. "Wow. It's hard to choose."

"Let's see the lights and then walk over to see the mansion. Okay?" Carlos suggested, leaning against her.

"I like that plan, because you know I never get tired of Christmas lights," she replied with a delighted grin.

"Exactly why I suggested we do both. I like seeing the happiness on your face when you're looking at them." Carlos gave her a quick kiss and grabbed her by the hand. "So let the fun continue."

Nedra felt a rush of bliss as he pulled her close against his body while they strolled the half block to the Tunnel of Lights display. Her heart soared as she replayed his words in her head. Carlos considered her preferences and wanted to please her. He didn't mind holding her hand in public or being close to her. According to her self-help relationship books, he showed all of the signs that his feelings were genuine. He didn't act as if being with her was optional.

For the rest of the evening they talked, laughed and even joined in the singing of holiday songs. Later they went to Nedra's apartment after picking up a late-night snack. Wrapped in a blanket on her sofa, they watched a movie until their closeness became too much of a temptation.

Making love to Carlos satisfied Nedra physically and emotionally. She felt sure he'd kissed and licked every inch of her body before entering her. His long, deliberate strokes pushed her over the edge until nothing else existed except intense pleasure. Afterwards, she didn't get that sinking feeling of mild regret as her lover hustled into his clothes to leave. Carlos stayed right by Nedra's side, talking for hours until they both drifted off to sleep.

"So this is what it feels like," Nedra said as sleep tugged at her eyelids. She snuggled closer to Carlos.

"Hmm?" he asked without opening his eyes.

"A perfect fit," Nedra whispered and yawned.

After a few seconds of silence, Carlos sighed and kissed her forehead. "Yeah."

\*\*\*\*

On Monday morning, Carlos was in the office of his shop located in the better part of town. Though Mid-City had its share of crime, unlike Easy Town, there were no daily shootings or robberies. He went through the spreadsheets, looking at his cash flow and expenses, and frowned at the results. The shop in Easy Town had taken a sales hit and business had gone down by thirty percent. Carlos grunted and stared at the figures. His business partner and friend, Brian Gaines, walked into the office and dropped into a chair.

"The look on your face doesn't signal good news, bru," said Brian. He took out his smartphone and glanced at it.

"The Easy Town shop is off; way off, man." Carlos clicked the wireless mouse to sync with his tablet. He'd be up late looking at the figures again at home.

"Having your business surrounded by six police cars will do that, bru," Brian replied with a grunt. He put his phone back in the case clipped to his belt.

"Not to mention video of an employee and two customers taking the perp walk in handcuffs downtown," Carlos added.

"Yeah, and shown on all three local TV stations. At least the reporters weren't in the 'hood the day the cops showed up at our store and our names weren't mentioned."

"Damn. This happened at the worst time." Carlos went back to studying the spreadsheet.

Brian shrugged. "Dude, there ain't a good time for being at the center of a criminal investigation, but at least your mama kept us both out of jail. Whew, that was close."

"I'm sorry I got you into this, man. I wouldn't blame you if you walked away. I've been seven different kinds of dumb – again." Carlos shook his head.

"I told you not to keep sweatin' it," Brian replied. "What our customers choose to do is not your responsibility."

"As my expensive lawyer argued so well," Carlos added with a twinge of guilt.

He had a very clear idea that his best customers were not law-abiding citizens with good jobs. They rolled up with lots of cash, talking rough and looking even rougher. Of course, his attorney had made the point that he hadn't stereotyped young black men, but Carlos knew the deal; so did his employees. Brian had even hired a couple from the neighborhood to act as unofficial bouncers. Six of the guys who came to the shop had a tendency to get into tense stand-offs. Carlos and Brian guessed they had beefs on the street. Several of the guys brought their equally tough-talking girlfriends inside. The women were just as likely to brawl; place and time didn't matter. They'd even curse in front of children and old people.

"We let things get out of hand, Brian. No, I let things get out of hand." Carlos tapped a fist on his the surface of his desk.

"What were you supposed to do, refuse to take their money? It was good money, too," Brian added with regret in his voice. "We expanded to selling rims, fancy hood ornaments and interior fix-ups. It was sweet."

Carlos shook his head. "Yeah, and all that fixing up included hiding money, drugs and drug-cooking equipment."

"Let's look on the bright side. We didn't go to jail. We can always work on bouncing back, and your mother managed to keep a lid on more *News at Eleven* stories. It's good to have connected parents and friends in high places." Brian pointed a forefinger at Carlos and stood up. "Listen, our strategy has worked. Getting a security service for the last six months and doing flyers were great ideas. People are starting to feel comfortable coming back. Remember when sales were down fifty percent?"

Carlos heaved a sigh. "You're right. Things could have gone much worse."

"Sales are slowly coming out of the hole, but it's going to take time."

"Yeah," replied Carlos, trying to see the bright side that Brian presented.

Brian's phone played the latest hit R&B song. He took the phone out of his hip case and glanced at the screen. "Here's another text from Keosha. Damn it, now what? Humph, more money. Big shock."

"You know, I could advance you on the next distribution of profits before the quarterly accounting period," Carlos offered, without asking if his colleague had caught up on his child-support payments.

"Nah, I got it handled. She just wants to yank my chain 'cause she knows I've got a new girlfriend. She has more ways of coming up with what the kid needs than she has hair in her weave." Brian snorted and scowled.

"New girlfriend, huh?" Carlos asked. "You've got two baby mamas and two kids already." He held up a palm when Brian shot a heated glance at him. "I'm not judging, just sayin'."

"I know, bru. Brittany is starting to drop hints about us living together and leaving bridal catalogues lying around. I'm thinking I need to move on." Brian lifted an eyebrow at Carlos. "Better stay alert for when your new lady starts in on you."

"Nedra doesn't play games and no dropping of hints. We're on the same page."

Brian grunted. "You better listen to your friend. *All* women play games, especially when it comes to hooking a man who owns his own business."

"Not Nedra. I'm not going to run from her. We feel... right." Carlos shrugged at his effort to find the right words without sounding corny.

"Oh no, bru, don't tell me the ultimate player is whipped. Wake up, dude, you've been hypnotized or something." Brian barked a loud laugh.

"Runnin' from woman to woman is old, man. They're all starting to blend together, just different color weaves and low-cut tops. I want somebody I can talk things over with; somebody I don't mind introducing to my kid." Carlos stood up. "We're closing in on forty. Five years to go."

"Quit talkin' crazy. Look, you're being sucked in by the holidays and all those mushy Christmas commercials. You know, families sitting around the tree eating sugar cookies and opening presents. Don't fall for it." Brian waved a hand at him. "After New Year's Day you'll snap out of it."

"I don't think so, man. I don't think so." Carlos smiled at the memory of being in Nedra's arms and feeling at home. "I didn't even have sense enough to know I was lonely," he added softly.

Brian had gone back to checking e-mails on his phone. "What?"

"Nothing, nothing; I'm just looking forward to the holidays. For one thing, I get Carly for Christmas this year." Carlos had managed to shake off the bad mood caused by looking at the spreadsheets.

"So you're playing the family man? Whatever floats your boat, bru." Brian shook his head. He put his phone away again and looked up. "So, Miss Nedra Wallace is cool about the whole unpleasantness with the cops? She doesn't mind about the community service and everything? That's one special lady."

Carlos rubbed his chin hard. His smile vanished and he cleared his throat. "Uh, yeah."

Brian cocked his head to one side. "She does know, right?"

"We're just getting to know each other and…"

Carlos shrugged.

"Bru, this is me you're talking to. You haven't brought it up because you don't know how she'll take it." Brian's eyes widened and he snapped his fingers. "Wait a minute. Her boss is running for office against the mayor."

"So?" asked Carlos, avoiding his gaze.

Brian laughed. "So!"

"Look, if things go to the next level…"

"You're talking about introducing her to your kid and the three of you being all cozy this Christmas. The next level is y'all making up the wedding invitation list. That is not a conversation you want to have at your engagement party." Brian slapped his thigh and fell against the chair laughing.

Carlos stared at him with a stony expression on his face. "Don't give up your day job to become a comedian. I know what I'm doing."

Brian finally stopped laughing and sat up straight. "You right, bru, the last thing you need is for that story to be put on blast. Your mama has an election next year and her pal, the mayor, could take a major political hit. Constable Davidson would love to use that against *both* of them."

"Nedra wouldn't tell her boss anything we discuss," Carlos stated.

"Yeah, but better safe than sorry," replied Brian, standing. "I agree with you."

"I didn't say…"

"I better get out of here; don't want to be late for my meeting with Cool Tools Inc. We can really enhance our business by partnering with them. I'll let you know how it goes." Brian walked around the desk and slapped Carlos on the back. "Keep your head up, partner. We're going to be better than ever."

"Sure, yeah." Carlos watched Brian leave. His

'holiday happy' mood had not lasted long. The spreadsheet seemed to mock him again.

Chapter 7

Three days later, Nedra attended a press conference called by a coalition of local law enforcement agencies. The Baton Rouge police chief, the East Baton Rouge sheriff and Nedra's boss were about to announce a new crime initiative. They had all gotten together to apply for a federal grant to fund a program to reduce crime in some of the worst neighborhoods.

Nedra was happy to be out of range of the four media cameras pointed at the podium. Constable Davidson stood in his dress uniform, chatting with the police chief and sheriff. All three were smiling and relaxed. The mayor stood apart from them with a stiff expression as he spoke to several parish council members. Reporters focused their attention on the whole group, watching their every gesture, expression and interaction; they knew of the animosity between the mayor and the constable.

Mayor Bates, known for being touchy and pugnacious, had used subtle means to sabotage the grant application process. Not because he didn't think it was a good idea, but because it wasn't his idea. Rod and the other law-enforcement leaders would be getting the credit, so face time with the media only annoyed him more. Because of the election, the mayor knew that blocking a crime-fighting effort would be bad for his image. Nedra watched as he finally joined the other three men. Nodding to them, he said a few words.

"Your boss is on a roll. He's got the holiday charity thing wrapped up and now this. Anybody would think he actually cares about people."

Nedra had been so intent on watching the four men that she hadn't seen Dwayne sidle up beside her. As his strong cologne swept over her like a choking fog, she inched as far away as possible without moving into camera view.

Nedra shot him a brief sideways glance and ignored his attempt to goad her. "Hello, Dwayne. Sheriff Berg and Chief White played a big part. This isn't just about Constable Davidson."

"Yeah, but the other two aren't running for office, at least not yet. I heard Berg is jockeying to be appointed to a big position with the state attorney general's office," Dwayne whispered, moving closer.

"Today is about making the city a safer place and saving lives, not politics," Nedra clipped before he could go on.

"Is that a line from your boss' speech? Good thing you're writing for him. Constable Davidson isn't exactly smooth when it comes to expressing himself before the cameras." Dwayne chuckled. "He'll have to brush up if he's going against the mayor next year."

"He'll be just fine," Nedra replied, unable to keep the edge out of her voice. Dwayne had a gift for testing her commitment to non-violence.

"Hey, don't take offense. Just because our bosses are political rivals doesn't mean we can't be friends." Dwayne's voice took on a wheedling sound. "I respect the guy. He's done some good things."

"This happens to be the *third* grant that Constable Davidson has helped win. Our office used a huge surplus to upgrade the city jail and he has reduced outstanding warrants by thirty percent." Nedra faced Dwayne. "Yeah, I'd say he's done 'some good things'."

He smiled at her. "Truce, lady. You've made your point. We have two worthy opponents. The election is months away and the constable hasn't confirmed that he'll even run for the senate seat. Neither of our bosses will care if we have lunch after this press conference. What do you say?"

"Dwayne, politics is not the reason I won't have lunch with you," Nedra whispered. A blonde woman standing on the other side of him seemed intent on reading their lips. When Nedra stared at her, she blinked rapidly and walked off.

"I've explained my situation. Okay, so you're kickin' it with Carlos Jacobs… for now." Dwayne's voice held a trace of irritation.

"He's single," Nedra tossed back and smiled.

"And he plans to stay that way for a long, long time. From what I hear, Carlos loves variety. Don't start having dreams of a picket fence, a dog and two-point-five kids; not with that dude."

"What I expect or don't expect is definitely none of your business. You should be concentrating on your wife and treating her right," she snapped, careful to keep her voice low. "And one more thing, stop bathing in cheap cologne."

Nedra spun around and marched to the other side of the room. The district attorney stepped up to the podium microphone a few seconds later and the crowd began to quiet down. The DA gave an overview of the new program, and then he and the other men answered questions from reporters. The mayor had little to say and didn't look at all pleased to be present. His expression stiffened when Constable Davidson began to speak.

When Rod stepped aside, the DA thanked him for suggesting the grant and the program. Mayor Bates glanced at the two men before staring at something in the distance. Nedra repressed a grin. Then she noticed Dwayne staring at her from across the room. An uneasy feeling took root in the pit of her stomach.

****

That afternoon, Nedra met with her boss to go over

his schedule and any other tasks they had. Constable Davidson seemed relaxed and in a good mood. After an hour they finished up, and he rocked his leather executive chair back while gazing out of the large window on the west wall of his office.

"The press conference went well, don't you think?" Rod asked. "But there's a lot of work ahead. In the next six months we should have staff in place though."

"Yes, sir," Nedra replied. She shifted in her chair and continued to make notes on her tablet computer.

"I just wish we had more cooperation from the mayor and his people. Still we did good getting this far." Rod rubbed his chin for a few seconds and looked at Nedra. "I've decided to run for the District Fifteen state senate seat. Senator Harrison has reached her term limit and she has been nudging me about running for the past year."

"Yes, sir, I think you'd do a great job, too," Nedra said sincerely.

Her boss had his faults, but despite his love of the limelight and political posturing at times, Rod Davidson got things done. Nedra had listed only a partial list of his accomplishments when goading Dwayne earlier.

"Thank you, Nedra. I appreciate your encouragement and competence. My office is working smoothly because of your excellent work. I don't have to worry about things getting done. That frees me to concentrate on big issues. I apologize for not saying so more often." Rod nodded at her with a solemn expression.

"Thank you, sir. I never doubted that you recognized my work." Nedra smiled back at him. Like most bosses, Rod only noticed when things didn't go well. She made it her business to make sure he didn't need to address the smaller details about the office.

"Technically, you could work on my campaign since

you're not a classified city employee, but we won't give my opponent any ammunition. We'll avoid even the appearance of impropriety."

"Yes, sir," Nedra replied.

She thought of how she had insulted Dwayne and imagined him seeking revenge for her words. Knowing him, he'd make digging up dirt on Rod or anything about the constable's office a special project.

"When I'm elected I hope you'll consider being my chief legislative assistant. I'll need good, level-headed support when I enter that pressure cooker." Rod sat taller in his chair as if he were already in office at the state capitol. "It'll be a tough election. Mayor Bates takes no prisoners when he runs a campaign, but I'm ready for him."

"Uh, Constable Davidson, I had a little, um, run in with the mayor's top assistant." Nedra stopped when her boss raised his hand like a traffic cop.

"Dwayne has been flirting with you. He has an inflated opinion of how charming he is to women. You set him straight and didn't sugar coat it. Am I right?" asked Constable Davidson with a chuckle.

"Yes sir. The thing is he has a bit of a mean streak." Nedra bit her bottom lip. "I shouldn't have let him get on my nerves. I sort of insulted him."

"I'm sure he deserved it."

"He did, but I may have given him even more incentive to go on a smear campaign. I just wanted you to know." Nedra let out a long sigh, relieved at getting it off her chest.

Her boss shook his head and grew serious. "You didn't need to give Dwayne any encouragement to look for ways to hit below the belt, trust me. He was planning to come after me long before you told him off; not to mention his boss and I haven't gotten along in years." Constable Davidson smiled again. "So, enjoy the memory of giving the jerk a verbal smackdown. I just hate that I wasn't close enough to see it."

"Yes sir." Nedra laughed with him.

"I can swing with the best of 'em, so Dwayne can bring it. If they want to go negative in the campaign, I'll be happy to hit back; not directly though. I know how to keep my hands clean even when the mud is slinging." Constable Davidson wore a determined expression as though anticipating the fight ahead.

"Okay then," Nedra replied and cleared her throat. She thought of Carlos and his mother's close ties to the mayor for the rest of the day.

*\*\*\**

Two days later, Nedra met Carlos for dinner at a seafood restaurant in Mid-City. The dining room was crowded for a Wednesday. The gray, rainy December weather hadn't seemed to dampen the good mood of the young professionals. Christmas garlands and lights added to the merry atmosphere.

Nedra arrived first and found a table away from the entrance to avoid the chilly air each time the door opened. She ordered a pot of hot tea and enjoyed the scenery outside the restaurant windows. Town Centre, an upscale shopping complex, had beautiful lights strung along its busy boulevard. Gigantic green, gold, red and deep purple gift boxes were positioned around the large trees that graced the intersections leading into the stores.

Carlos arrived twenty minutes past their agreed upon time of six thirty. Night had fallen and the headlights from passing cars lit up the street. Nedra watched him stride in wearing a khaki rain jacket over a handsome chocolate-brown pullover sweater and matching slacks. Brushing a few rain drops from his sleeves, he scanned the room until he found her.

"Sorry you had to wait, baby," said Carlos. "Things are a little bit hectic at the shops. I swear, everybody in town must be trying to get their cars dressed up for the holidays. We're selling rims and accessories like they're going out of style." He kissed Nedra's cheek and sat down.

"No problem. My day got kind of crazy as well. I'm winding down with some of this delicious tea. Want a cup?" Nedra signaled to the waiter.

"I'm a manly man. I need coffee," Carlos replied with a grin.

"Oh, please." Nedra rolled her eyes and giggled.

They ordered and the waiter hurried off to take care of the other customers.

"Dang, I thought this wouldn't be such a busy night." Carlos glanced around at the throng of people eating, ordering, leaving and arriving.

"People are shopping, honey." Nedra nodded to the diners sat at several tables nearby. Large shopping bags sat on the floor at their feet. "I've only just about finished. I'm waiting for toys to be delivered from Toy Central for my nephews and nieces."

"Cutting it close, huh? Christmas is a week away." Carlos sat back as the waiter placed a cup of steaming coffee in front of him, before racing off again.

"Yeah, I've been so busy with work and everything. The customer service rep at Toy Central assured me that I would get the delivery this week; Friday at the latest. I'm hoping my neighbor has them for me when I get home," said Nedra, holding up crossed fingers. "Last year, I foolishly waited too late to order and ended up at the store on the Saturday before Christmas Day. Never again."

Carlos started to laugh again and then stopped. He held his head in both hands. "Crap."

Nedra raised her eyebrows at him. "You do have

your baby girl's Christmas gifts, right? She'll be here in three days."

"I kept putting it off, and things got so wild at both my shops. I have some clothes and a doll, but I was supposed to get her these electronic bugs. She wants them so bad." Carlos looked at Nedra with desperation stamped on his handsome face. "You've got to help me."

She shook her head. "Oh no, I'm not going into a toy store this late in the game. Those places are like war zones."

"Please, baby. Please. I can either be a hero daddy or scar my little girl for life," Carlos blurted out. "Tell you what, let's go to my place and search the internet for them. I still have time to pay extra for emergency shipping."

"If those bug things haven't sold out," Nedra said.

Carlos blinked at her. "Don't even say it! If we can't get them online Friday, we can go to…"

"Uh-huh. You got yourself into this mess. I've still got the scars from last Christmas when I tried to beat three grandmothers to the last three electronic car tracks we all wanted. Those little elderly ladies were cold-blooded killers." Nedra shook her head.

Carlos grabbed her hand and squeezed it. "Please, baby."

She continued to shake her head at him. "Start praying to the online-shopping angels, sweetie."

All through dinner they enjoyed pretending to argue. Nedra laughed at the way Carlos grew frantic every time she reminded him of the date, and he promised her whatever she wanted on the condition that she helped him brave Toy Central. By the time they finished eating, Nedra's sides hurt from laughing at the panicked father.

"In all seriousness, I love the way you take being a father seriously. A lot of men don't even visit their kids, let alone have them over for Christmas. If you tell me you comb Carly's hair on your own, that's it and I'll help you out." Nedra grinned at him.

Carlos sat up straight and patted his chest in pride. "I've been styling Carly's hair since she was crawling. I even painted her little fingernails and toenails a few times." Then he dropped his voice and glanced around. "Uh, let's keep that between us. Not even my best friend, Brian, knows about the polish stuff. He teases me enough about being a family man."

Nedra melted at the image of Carlos lovingly putting ribbons in his child's hair. "That's beautiful, Carlos, really."

He shrugged and blushed at the compliment. "Well, I call it our bonding time. So, you see why I have to bring my A game when she visits."

"Then we better get on our job and find those bugs. By the way, what exactly are these things and why do kids love them?" Nedra patted her lips with a large paper napkin.

"They're actually neat. You've got a spider, a caterpillar and a beetle. They crawl around and change direction if they bump into anything." Carlos' eyes lit up as if he were a kid describing what he wanted for Christmas.

Nedra raised an eyebrow. "Um, are you sure they're for Carly? You sound suspiciously excited about getting your hands on them."

"Ah, now you know the benefits of parenthood. You have a good cover for playing with cool toys." He grinned back at her. "No, we're not splitting the tab this time. It's the holidays and I'm treating both my girls."

"You mean bribing me to help pull your butt out of a tight spot," Nedra wisecracked. Still, she shivered at his reference to them as a family.

"That too," Carlos replied and hooked an arm around her waist.

They left the restaurant and went to his apartment. Within minutes of being inside, they were sat at his computer, searching. Three websites later, it became clear that finding the little bugs was going to be a huge challenge. Forty minutes into their quest, they took a break.

Nedra nestled against Carlos' solid chest as they sat on his sofa. "Don't freak. I think we'll find them," she said.

"I hope so." He heaved a sigh. "The last thing I need is my mother hounding me about waiting until the last minute." He was about to go on when his cell phone rang. "Hello. Yeah, what's up? Outside? Right now? But I thought... Fine. It's all about you."

"Everything okay?" asked Nedra, feeling a foreboding at the scowl on Carlos' handsome face.

"Chanté has decided to bring Carly early for her visit," he replied. "She's going on a ski trip with her latest man and they want to leave tomorrow. They're here." He tossed his cell phone on the sofa and stood.

"Here?" Nedra echoed. Just as the full impact of his words hit, the doorbell rang.

"Yeah and Chanté knows I won't kick about it. I don't want Carly to think she's done something wrong or that I don't want to see her." Carlos took a deep breath and let it out. A second later, he walked to the front door.

Nedra hurriedly smoothed down her turtleneck and hair as she stood.

Carlos opened the door and his daughter literally jumped into his arms. As he kissed her and made a big fuss over how cute she looked, a statuesque woman with auburn hair watched. Chanté was about to speak when she noticed Nedra. Stepping around Carlos and Carly, she entered the living room.

"Sorry to interrupt your *intimate* evening. I'm

Chanté Epperson." The woman gave Nedra a cool appraisal from head to toe as she spoke. When she smiled, her even, white teeth looked ready to bite.

"Hello," was all Nedra trusted herself to say. She was determined not to play war games. Nor was she willing to be part of a stereotype: the baby mama versus new girlfriend drama.

"Ooh, I get to hug and kiss you extra days," said Carlos as he kissed Carly's cute milk-chocolate cheek for the fourth time.

"Who's that, daddy?" she asked, pointing to Nedra. Carly had obviously picked up on her mother's vibe.

Carlos didn't miss a beat, and Chanté watched his response with intensity. "Come over here and meet Miss Nedra," he said. "She's a very special lady."

Carly eyed her with curiosity. "Hi."

Nedra smiled. "Hello, it's so nice to meet you. Your daddy is super proud of you."

"Thank you." Carly wrapped a little arm around Carlos' neck and blinked at Nedra shyly.

"So you know all about us. Tell us about you," Chanté said with a feline smile.

"I work for the city constable here and I'm old Baton Rouge," Nedra replied promptly and smiled back at her. "Born and bred in the Red Stick."

"Old Baton Rouge family, huh? I bet Judge Jacobs loves that." Chanté shot Carlos a sideways glance as she murmured the last sentence.

"Do you sit up high and tell people what to do, like my Meemee?" Carly blinked at Nedra.

"No, Nedra isn't a judge like your grandmother, sweetheart. You hungry?" asked Carlos, smoothing down a stray hair that had come loose from one of the little girl's two thick braids.

"We ate. You think I don't make sure Carly eats healthy," Chanté shot back with a brief look of annoyance.

"I had chicken fingers dipped in honey mustard sauce, fries and a biscuit. I didn't eat the biscuit though. Too greasy." Carly spoke matter-of-factly, undoing her mother's defensive response.

"Here, go put your suitcase in whatever corner you'll be sleeping in, since daddy has company." Chanté extended a pink, child-size, rolling duffle bag.

"Okay." Carly climbed down from her father's embrace and looked up at him.

"You'll be in your bedroom, like always, honey," said Carlos, smiling at his daughter. When she grinned and darted up the stairway, singing, he turned back to her mother.

Chanté seemed unaffected by his cold expression. "I can take her to your mama's house if she's in the way."

"Carly is never 'in the way'. Thank you," Carlos replied quietly.

"Just sayin'…" Chante was about to go on when her phone chimed. She took it out and read the text. Seconds later, she tapped a short response and put it away. "I'll give Carly a last goodbye kiss."

"Uh-huh." Carlos looked away.

As Chanté disappeared up the staircase, Nedra put a hand on Carlos' shoulder. "You okay?"

He sighed. "Is it that obvious that she was working on my last damn nerve?"

"Kinda," Nedra whispered.

She was about to say more when Chanté appeared at the top of the stairs, gazing down at them. "Well, she seems to be settling in with all the goodies you have stocked up there," she announced, walking downstairs. She glanced at them both, and appeared to notice how close they stood. "Merry Christmas," she added.

"Same to you, and enjoy your trip," Nedra said quickly. She could feel the simmering anger radiating from Carlos.

"Thank you. Bye, Carlos." Chanté flashed him a flirtatious smile.

"Bye." Carlos walked to the door, pulled it open, and shut it firmly after his ex had left.

Nedra wondered if the two of them were really over. "She still gets to you."

Carlos wrapped both arms around Nedra. "Not in a good way. She wants to fight, even though it isn't good for our child. Notice how she tries to subtly make Carly think I might not have room for her in my life?"

"Daddy, do we have any praline ice cream?" Carly yelled from upstairs. "I'm hungry."

Carlos' tense expression eased at the sound of her voice. "Baby girl, I thought you ate."

"Yeah, but I didn't have dessert."

"I can't argue with that logic," he said, laughing. "Come on down here. I happen to have your favorite."

"Look, I'll go," suggested Nedra, walking towards the hall closet to get her coat.

"No way! After I put her to bed, we need to search for you-know-what." Carlos kept his voice low as Carly bounced down the steps.

The girl glanced at Nedra and then at her father. "Mommy says I should stay in my room so I won't be any trouble, 'cause you have company."

"You're never any trouble. We're going to all have ice cream." Carlos walked over to Nedra and closed the closet door. "Right?"

"Right," agreed Nedra. She felt a nervous flutter at the probing gaze of Carly's light brown eyes.

They settled into Carlos' breakfast nook over bowls of ice cream. Unlike her mother, Carly seemed more curious than hostile towards Nedra. She had the sweetest little girl, charm-school manners. When Carly began to yawn, Carlos decided to take her upstairs to bed. She waved as he carried her. "Goodnight, Miss Nedra."

Nedra felt a tug at her heart strings. "Sleep tight, sweetie."

She returned to the computer and searched for the elusive robotic bug toys that everyone had to have. Twenty minutes later, Carlos came back down. He'd changed into a T-shirt and sweat pants, with the Southern University jaguar mascot on both.

"She's already dozing off. Let's give it another five minutes to be sure and then back to the hunt." Carlos sighed and sat next to Nedra.

"She's so lovely, Carlos." Nedra felt a jab of sadness at what she'd been missing all these years.

"We're going to have a great Christmas together; the three of us." Carlos kissed her and held her tightly.

"Yes, we will," replied Nedra, looking forward to the holidays in a way she never had before.

## Chapter 8

Tuesday night, Nedra sang *The Twelve Days of Christmas* as she cooked dinner. Carlos arrived just as she was putting the spaghetti and spicy meatballs on simmer. She rushed to check the garlic bread and then scurried to her front door as the bell chimed a second time.

"Be patient, man, I'm coming," Nedra called as she flipped the locks.

"I'm hungry. Please let me in!" Carlos groaned. When she swung the door wide, he stood pretending to slump against the door. He reached out to her. "Don't know if I can make it."

She grabbed his arm and yanked him through the doorway. "Oh please. Come on in here before my neighbors call the police."

Carlos locked the door, inhaled and exhaled. "Something smells so good."

Nedra hurried back to the oven. The edges of the bread had started to turn light brown. She removed the tray and turned off the oven. "Spicy meatballs, my secret sauce and pasta," she said. "Oh and garlic bread. With all those carbs, I doubt we'll have room for dessert."

"I'm hoping for spice alright." Carlos winked at her and did a dance turn to the music coming from Nedra's sound system.

"Getting fresh already, huh? Besides, you're in daddy mode. Best behave. I don't want your family saying you left your daughter behind because of me. You could have brought Carly."

"Actually, it's tradition," he replied. "She spends at least one night with my parents. They love having her over. My niece and nephews go over as well, and my sister spends the night to help out."

Carlos broke off a corner of garlic bread and Nedra tapped him on the hand. "Stop that. We'll be sitting down in a minute," she said. "The table is set."

"I couldn't resist. Garlic bread is like an aphrodisiac, by the way." Carlos came up behind Nedra and kissed her neck.

She giggled as his hands roamed over her hips and thighs. "Don't mess with the cook during food preparation. I think that's a health law or something."

"I wouldn't want to do anything illegal, at least not yet." Carlos swatted her butt and went to the sink to wash his hands. "I'll get the bread and salad."

"Good, put those wandering hands to good use," Nedra wisecracked.

"I will later on." Carlos wiggled his eyebrows at her.

They shared jokes and laughter for the next hour over dinner. Nedra marveled at how different this holiday would be from the previous one. Another break-up, just before Christmas, had left her feeling down last year. Her friends maintained that trifling men always got the goods and skipped out before the holidays to avoid gift giving. Nedra was feeling much less cynical this year. After dinner they sat on her sofa to relax.

"So how's your visit with Carly going so far?" asked Nedra.

"Great, as always. We had a talk about you though."

Nedra froze and stared at him. "You talked about me?"

"She wanted to know if you were my girlfriend and if you would be moving in with me, and…"

Nedra's mouth dropped open. "She's only five! How could she even think up such questions?"

"Well, for one thing, her mama has had a few 'boyfriends' since we split up. I'm sure her mother has spoken about my dating habits and not in a good way either." Carlos sighed. "Our break-up was messy."

"And Carly saw and heard a lot?"

"Yeah, Chanté isn't shy about speaking her mind in front of our kid," he replied. "In case you've heard any gossip, she didn't catch me with another woman in our bedroom. She told everyone that to make herself look sympathetic. I found out she was sexing the assistant pastor at her church. He was supposedly 'counseling' her on our marriage issues."

Carlos nodded when Nedra stared at him in shock. She blinked rapidly. "Whoa. Gotta let that one sink in for a minute."

"The church hushed it up and I'd never blast out that kind of news about the mother of my child. Since we're talking about relationships, the gossip you heard about me having lots of ladies is true." Carlos cleared his throat. "I never lied to any of them though. They were told upfront that I wasn't looking for a live-in, let alone a wife."

"I see." Nedra stared ahead at the wall-mounted flat screen, even though it wasn't turned on. She had been leaning into Carlos, but now she sat straight.

"Hey, where you goin'? I was talking about *them*. I see us together, for a long time," he said softly. "That's why I wanted you to know."

Nedra smiled as he pulled her close to his body. "I wasn't picking out furniture for us or anything," she said. Still, she savored the warmth from his solid arm around her.

"Honey, other women have met Carly briefly. None of them spent the holidays with us." Carlos kissed her. "You and me, we're together. Got it?"

"Got it." Nedra could barely catch her breath. The look in his eyes made her tremble. Then she gasped, "We're serving dinner Christmas day, remember? You know we start early prepping the site. Fortunately, we have more than enough volunteers this year. You stay home with baby girl. Christmas morning is a big deal for kids."

"Carly gets up at the crack of dawn to tear open her gifts. I'll bring her with me. I think the experience will be great for her. I won't be able to stay for hours after though." Carlos rubbed his chin.

"If you're sure, then we'd be glad to have her. We have school kids who help all the time. And I agree, kids should learn about giving to others. Did I mention that you're a wonderful father?" Nedra kissed him long and passionately.

"Yes, but I won't complain about more compliments from you," Carlos replied softly once the kiss ended.

"Come with me, daddy…"

Nedra tugged him to his feet and started down the hall to her bedroom. She felt resistance and glanced over her shoulder. Carlos pulled his sweater over his head and took off his slacks in record time. He yanked her to him and put a hand under her blouse. Nedra gasped as his large thumb rubbed her nipple hard. He kissed her.

"What's wrong with right here?" he whispered, his lips still pressing against hers.

He lovingly undressed Nedra, still whispering everything he liked about her curves and the way she smelled. Her senses whirled out of control as his body pressed against hers. Within seconds he lifted her and set her on the edge of the sofa back. As he entered her, Nedra cried out. Their lovemaking started out in frenzy as they tore at each other, hungrily. No tender, taking their time this night. Instead, they clung to each other as though they'd been apart for weeks. In sync, they reached the blissful moment that left them both moaning and trembling. Nedra panted as they both grew still.

"I hope your neighbors don't complain to the management. I might have gotten a little loud for a minute." Carlos shuddered and lifted Nedra from the sofa.

"Fortunately, we have great sound proofing," she gasped.

They padded down the hallway to her bedroom and climbed beneath the bed covers.

"Good to know," Carlo mumbled, his eyes closing as he nuzzled Nedra's hair. "I love that shampoo."

"Green apple and ginger," she replied. Then she snapped out of her daze. "Shouldn't you check in with your folks to see if everything is okay?"

"Nope, they're fine. Besides, they'll call my cell if they need me." He shifted to fit his body against hers.

Nedra caressed his cheek with a finger. "Honey?"

"Umm?" His eyes were still closed.

"Thanks for being so open and honest with me, for sharing your life. I love that you trust me." Nedra smiled at him.

Carlos opened his eyes and looked at her for a few seconds. "I'm in love with you, Nedra. Believe me?"

She laughed as tears slid down her face. Nedra couldn't speak at first. She kissed him with a desire that had nothing to do with sex; her heart beating hard enough to disturb the neighbors in spite of the sound proofing. He rested his head on her breasts and Nedra kissed the top of his head.

"Yes, I do. I love you back, Carlos Jacobs."

\*\*\*\*

Wednesday morning, Carlos left Nedra's apartment and stopped by his place briefly to change clothes. He wouldn't dare to pick up his daughter wearing the same shirt and pants as he'd worn the night before. His mother would definitely give him 'the look' and Carly would most likely question him in front of the rest of the family. She was like her mother, always ready to say what was on her mind, whenever and wherever.

Once he'd changed into a dark blue sweater and jeans, Carlos headed over to the upscale neighborhood where his parents lived. Once he'd parked his Accura, he headed into the house and made for the kitchen. His mother was sitting at the long, marble-topped breakfast bar, nursing a mug of hot cocoa. She stared into the cup with a frown, as though searching for a solution to a problem.

"Good morning," said Carlos. He walked over and kissed her right cheek, before sitting down on a stool.

Yvonne looked up after a few moments. She drained her cup and walked over to the double kitchen sink. "How was your evening the other night with Ms. Wallace and Carly?"

Carlos suppressed a sigh at the interrogation he knew was coming. "I'm sure you heard the details from Carly already, Mother."

"I want the adult perspective. Carly hasn't made up her mind yet what she thinks of your new lady friend." Yvonne meticulously washed and dried the mug, and placed it on a decorative wooden rack, which held five more matching mugs.

"We got along just fine as a matter of fact. We had ice cream and Carly asked a few questions. I'm sure she'll have more when we get together next time." Carlos grabbed a ceramic mug, went to the fancy brew machine, and filled half of it. Leaning against the counter, he waited.

"I see. You have an itinerary already." Yvonne wiped her hands on a large paper towel as she gazed at him.

"We're going to the Christmas Village, across the river in New Roads, Saturday night. Carly will get a big kick out of it and so will Nedra. She's like a little girl herself when it comes to Christmas lights and decorations." Carlos smiled and sipped the rich liquid.

"Is she now? How sweet," Yvonne said in a dry tone.

Carlos sipped again. "Okay, let's get it over with."

Yvonne gave him a poker-faced look. "What are you talking about?"

"You have something on your mind about Nedra and Carly. So let's just get to it while we're alone."

Yvonne crossed to a bar stool and sat down. "Not that it's any of my business. You're grown and have the right to parent my grandchild how you choose."

"Yes, indeed."

His mother squinted at him. "But you said yourself that Nedra might not be in your life for long. I understand you weren't expecting them to meet so fast. We have Chanté to thank for that."

"Chanté loves acting on impulse, usually to meet her own needs," Carlos replied.

"I see she hasn't changed much." Yvonne's frown deepened at the thought of her former daughter-in-law. "But, back to the subject. Maybe you shouldn't have them spend so much holiday time together. Carly is at a critical age. You wouldn't want her to start forming an attachment only to have the woman disappear."

Carlos raised an eyebrow at her mother. "I don't think Carly will be traumatized if we break up later. But not to worry, Mother, Nedra is not going to disappear anytime soon."

Yvonne lifted her chin. "Things are getting serious so soon? You hardly know her, son."

"We're spending time together to get to know each other. Besides, Nedra is exactly who I thought she'd be; smart, classy and unselfish. She was pretty good with Carly, too." Carlos smiled at his mother.

Yvonne didn't smile back. "I see."

"You're supposed to say, 'That's wonderful son. I'm glad you're happy'."

His mother looked at him intently. "I'm up for re-election in another two years. I'm also working on getting a federal judgeship appointment. Do you know what that means?"

"Yes, I do." Carlos gazed out of the bay window over the kitchen sink. The weather outside was crisp, with a clear blue sky and sunshine. His mother longed for the prestige of being on the federal bench.

"I want to preside over cases with national implications. Getting a spot on the Appeals Court might be out of reach. Rodney Davidson and his crew have blocked me, but I still have a chance at one of the district judgeships. At least two of the current judges are talking about retiring in another year or two."

Carlos glanced at his mother. Her eyes gleamed at the prospect of moving closer to her goal. He didn't need to ask how she knew about two federal judges considering retirement. Yvonne Elliot Jacobs had contacts in a lot of places. She helped lawyers and recent law-school graduates to get jobs with that in mind.

"Sounds great, Mother," he said, looking back out at the lovely weather. He pushed himself away from the counter and started for the sink.

"Just leave the mug there. I'll wash it," his mother said.

"Thanks. I'll get Carly and…"

"Carlos, I can't afford any kind of bad publicity, not with what's at stake. I've worked hard to get where I am. Davidson would be dancing in the streets downtown if he could use anything against me and the mayor." Yvonne's contralto voice went deeper as she made her point.

"Nedra and I are building trust, and getting closer. I don't want to keep any secrets from her," Carlos said quietly.

"Every relationship is based on at least a few little lies," Yvonne replied. "I don't want you to start feeling all sentimental and put my career goals at risk. Getting a federal nod is a delicate situation. One whisper of even the appearance of wrongdoing..."

Carlos crossed his arms. "Nedra wouldn't discuss anything shared between us."

"Really? You have a track record of getting bored quickly and moving on to the next woman. Nedra will then have a way to get back at you for dumping her," Yvonne said, standing.

Carlos sighed. How could he explain a set of emotions he'd never experienced before? He saw Nedra in his future. Still he tried. "Okay, I know you're skeptical. I've had a few girlfriends before, but this feels different. No, it *is* different."

"She works for Rod Davidson, Carlos," his mother hissed, as though that fact should be enough to make him understand.

He looked at his mother steadily. "We're not going to keep having this discussion. Nedra wouldn't tell her boss, even if she became angry with me. She's just not that kind of woman."

"At least wait a few months. Get to know her better before you start confessing your every mistake." Yvonne took a step towards him. "Do it for me."

Carlos let out a long sigh. "Fine, and I'll let you know when I do tell Nedra about the diversion program and my community service."

"Well that's something at least." Yvonne waved a hand.

"I'm going to take Carly to the office with me, and then we'll go Christmas shopping," he added, heading out of the kitchen.

"Oh, I didn't mention it," Yvonne said casually.

"Carly went with your father and the other kids for breakfast, and to shop for your present. Why not come back after work to get her?" She took the mug that Carlos had used and went to the sink.

Played smoothly, he thought, watching his mother. He realized that Yvonne purposely failed to mention that Carly wasn't even in the house so she could have a little chat. Carlos let out a gruff laugh and pulled out his car keys. "I'll be back around five o'clock."

"Sounds good, son. Have a good day." Yvonne smiled and offered her cheek.

Carlos shook his head and gave her a dutiful peck. "I'm sure you'll end up on the federal bench, Judge Jacobs."

Carlos left and drove towards his Mid-City shop first, his mother's words still running through his head.

**\*\*\*\***

Nedra heard the tinkle of her smartphone, signaling a text from Carlos. He had accepted her invitation to cook dinner tonight, as she'd known he would. The fixings for oven-fried chicken and creamy cheese pasta were waiting in her kitchen, and she planned to stop by a deli downtown to get some fresh-baked French bread on her way home.

"Well, well. Judging by the big smile on your face, I'm guessing you're having a good day." Gaylynn plopped down in one of the chairs in Nedra's office. "Glad somebody is happy. My supervisor is on the warpath over some mistakes. Thankfully, I didn't make them, but we're all suffering."

"Too bad she doesn't have the Christmas spirit." Nedra adjusted a small angel on the corner of her desk until she was satisfied with its position. She hummed a few bars of *Jingle Bells*. "Tis the season to spread love and joy."

"Well, I have to say that in her position I'd be in a bad mood, too, but she'll get over it," Gaylynn replied and then watched Nedra for few seconds. "At least it's Wednesday; hump day. Getting closer to a long weekend. That big ol' smile isn't because you've got the holiday spirit. I think it's because you had certain fine man in you, and not long ago."

"Don't be crude," Nedra tossed back, but kept smiling. "I'm in a great mood because I love Christmas."

"Uh-huh," Gaylynn snorted. "So what's new with the happy couple?"

"Well, we're going to the Christmas Village in New Roads Saturday. Carlos' little girl is in town and..."

"Oh-oh." Gaylynn shook her head.

Nedra frowned at her sister. "What's that supposed to mean?"

"You're going to play the wicked stepmother. Probably would be better if he had a boy child. Girls hate sharing daddy with strange women. I know my baby, Misha, would give a stepmother the blues. She ain't sharing Pierre with anybody. I'm lucky she lets me be with him." Gaylynn laughed.

"Carlos and I are still in the 'getting to know you' phase. But it's sweet of him to include me in his plans with Carly." Nedra smiled at the memory of seeing them together.

"Cute name. Now don't try to play your little sis, Nedra. You've got a 'seriously in love' glow about you. Based on him making all these plans for the holidays with you, I'm guessing you bagged the infamous Carlos Jacobs. Players do settle down." Gaylynn winked at her.

Nedra shrugged. "You know, I don't doubt that Carlos has been a player when it comes to women. He's so fine and runs a successful business."

"You got that right. He has what women want:

looks, money, and connections. We haven't talked about the bedroom yet." Gaylynn wiggled her eyebrows at Nedra.

"No. Don't even ask." Nedra squinted back.

Gaylynn gave a dramatic sigh. "Dang, that tells me enough. The man is good. Girl can't even find the words."

Nedra laughed at her sister. "Hush."

"I'm happy for you. The Wallace girls deserve some happiness. Despite what Mama says, Pierre loves the family thing. In fact, we're shopping for our wedding rings," said Gaylynn, grinning.

"What?" Nedra sprang to her feet, rushed around her desk and hugged Gaylynn tight. "This is like the best Christmas gift ever. Misha is going to be the prettiest little flower girl."

Gaylynn beamed at her. "I know. But we're going to keep it simple. We've set the date: June eighth, next year. Of course, you're going to be a bridesmaid."

"Uh, that goes without saying. I'd turn that wedding out if you didn't let me be in the wedding party," Nedra joked. Then she grew serious. "What did Jarae say?"

Gaylynn sighed. "I haven't told her yet."

"She's going to be happy for you. I know she will."

"Oh, I know," she replied. "It's just that she gets so bitter and down. I want to enjoy the happiness for a little while. Mama will be thrilled, but, of course, she'll say, 'It's about damn time; eight years and two kids later'."

Nedra laughed hard. Gaylynn did such an excellent imitation of Darcie Lee. "Girl, stop it. My face is hurting."

The sisters exchanged Darcie Lee stories and gasped for air between giggles. After a while, Gaylynn tapped Nedra on the shoulder and pointed. Dwayne stood in the open office doorway gazing at them. Nedra grabbed a tissue from the box on her desk and wiped her eyes.

"I need some water," said Gaylynn. She went to the pitcher on a side table and poured herself a cup. "Oo-wee, that was a good laugh. Hi, and excuse us."

"No problem. It's nice to see two beautiful women having a good time." Dwayne strolled into Nedra's office and gave Gaylynn a head-to-toe glance.

"Dwayne, this is my younger sister, Gaylynn." Nedra wanted to slap the leer off his face. *Just like any predator, always on the prowl.* "This is Dwayne Grover, the mayor's confidential assistant."

"Nice to meet you," said Gaylynn, taking a sip of water. "Let me get back to my office. I'll call you later, sis."

"Sure thing." Nedra waved goodbye and faced Dwayne. She rolled her eyes as he stared at Gaylynn's butt as she walked away.

"*Very* nice meeting you, Gaylynn," called Dwayne. He seemed about to smack his lips, but then he pivoted his attention back to Nedra and smiled. "So you're in a good mood for the holidays, I see."

"Yes, as a matter of fact. What can I do for you?" Nedra moved back behind her desk. She didn't sit, but crossed her arms and looked at him.

"I just stopped by to wish you a Merry Christmas. Are you coming to the Gala?" Seeming not to notice Nedra's less than warm reception, Dwayne perched on the edge of her desk.

Nedra knew that Mayor Bates hosted a fancy Christmas party each year, held at a banquet hall that was owned and operated by his brother. An invitation to these parties was a hot ticket. He didn't skimp on food or entertainment, and guests had a chance to meet powerful and influential people.

Nedra realized that Dwayne's gaze had settled on open files. Scooping up the stack of papers on her desk, she replied, "No, I have other plans."

"Right, you're still kickin' it with Carlos Jacobs. The so-called *volunteer* and all-round good guy," replied Dwayne, barking a raspy chuckle.

Her temper boiled up. "Okay, what is your problem, Dwayne?"

"I don't like phony dudes. At least with me you'd know what you've got." Dwayne leaned forward and pointed at her.

"Yes, a cheating, married man who only thinks about himself. And you have the nerve to slam somebody else. Please." Nedra raked him with a gaze of scorn.

Dwayne stood and smoothed down the front of his expensive, brown-tweed sport jacket. "At least I'm not a criminal doing community service to keep my ass out of jail." He gave a nasty smirk when Nedra blinked at him. "Yeah, you heard me. Your lover man didn't volunteer to be at the Thanksgiving Holiday Hospitality dinner. His mama, the judge, worked a deal to get him out of serious trouble; something to do with drugs and guns. Why don't you ask Mr. Right? You have a *very* Merry Christmas."

Nedra's heart hammered in her chest as she watched Dwayne stroll out of her office. Without turning around, he waved a hand as he continued to chuckle. The roaring in her ears didn't block out the sound of his glee at having dropped a bomb on her.

Rod came out his office and patted her shoulder. "Nedra, are you okay?"

"Sir?" Nedra swallowed hard. She couldn't look away from the space where Dwayne had just stood.

Her boss glanced at the fancy wall clock. "Look, it's almost eleven. Since you were leaving at noon anyway, you can go now. Tracy can handle the office."

"I... I don't think..." Nedra fought against the feeling that there was a deep, dark hole opening up beneath her feet.

"Not much is happening since most folks took the day off. Go ahead and start your long holiday weekend. It's fine." Rod gave her a fatherly pat on the shoulder.

"Yes, sir," Nedra said.

Rod started for his office, but hesitated. "You sure I can't help?"

"No, I'm okay. Thanks." Nedra sorted through several folders on her desk. Placing them back into a file cabinet in a corner of her office, she locked it.

"Merry Christmas," Rod said quietly as he left.

"Same to you."

Nedra could not bring herself to repeat his words; not when her Christmas looked to be the very opposite of merry. She suddenly lost interest in the routine of leaving her desk neatly arranged. Purse on her shoulder, she marched out of the office building with no thought of last-minute shopping or decorating.

## Chapter 9

Carlos hummed along with a jazzy version of *No Place Like Home for the Holidays* as he sat in his office. He glanced at a new picture of Carly. Dressed in a pretty red dress, she sat in Santa's lap. The photo had been taken the night before at the Town Centre shopping mall. With a smile at the memory of how much fun they'd had, Carlos went back to reviewing the payroll records.

Brian came in and snapped his fingers to the music. "Man, I'm going to the mayor's Red Stick Gala. If I'm lucky, those fine twin nieces of his will be there, Tasha and Sasha, wow-wee!"

"Do you even know the true meaning of this holiday? It's about love." Carlos didn't look up from his task, but shook his head.

"That's what I'm sayin'. I'm more than willing to spread it around." Brian shook his hips and bobbed his head to the beat.

"I'm pretty sure we're talking about two different kinds of love, man." Carlos continued to verify the electronic time records on his computer.

"Hey, don't try to spoil my jam just 'cause you've decided on the ball and chain. I'm still free to mingle. I'd tell you to come and take one of the twins, but Nedra will probably be there." Brian pulled a long face.

"Nedra won't be there." Carlos scrolled to another screen as he answered.

Brian nodded with a grin. "Perfect. Your folks can babysit and we can rock with the twins. Just like the old days, huh? Damn, we had good times in college."

"Nedra won't be there because we'll be together Saturday night. We're taking Carly to the Christmas Village display. The Pointe Coupee historical society has

Main Street in New Roads decorated like an eighteenth century small town." Carlos glanced at Carly's photo again. "They're going to love it."

"How touching," replied Brian, pretending to wipe a tear from the corner of his eye. "Maybe I'll give up rockin' one of the twins and meet y'all over there. Hmm, let me think… hell no."

"You need help," Carlos shot back.

"You have your idea of holiday good times and I have mine. My stomach is talking to me. Want to get some lunch from The Po-boy Shoppe?" Brian turned towards the office door and stopped short. "Well, hello."

Nedra nodded to him and then transferred her gaze to Carlos. "Hello. Sorry if I'm interrupting a meeting."

Carlos got up from his chair and crossed the room to Nedra. He kissed her forehead and grabbed her by the hand. "Come on in, baby. This is my partner in crime, Brian Gaines."

"Nice to meet you," said Nedra. She gave Brian a polite smile that soon faded.

"You got here at just the right time. We were talking about lunch," Carlos added.

"We need to talk, Carlos."

Brian cocked an eyebrow them. "Uh, I'll catch you later, bru."

Carlos glanced at him briefly. "Okay." After Brian left, he turned back to Nedra and noticed her troubled expression. "What's wrong, babe. You sound all serious. Don't tell me you started cooking early and burned dinner." He laughed.

"When did you decide to make a fool of me, Carlos? That's all I want to know." Nedra's voice trembled, but then she seemed to gather strength. Her expression became rock hard as she stared at him.

"Where did that come from?"

"What was the exact moment? Did you size me up

as a desperate, single woman at the Holiday Hospitality dinner or was it when we met for coffee that first time?" Nedra pulled her hand free, adjusted her leather purse on one shoulder and crossed her arms.

"I have no idea what you're talking about, Nedra. Look, if I did something to upset you…"

Nedra cut him off. "Upset me? That doesn't begin to describe how I feel."

"I can tell you how I feel – confused as hell. I didn't decide to make a fool out of you, as you put it, and I'd appreciate an explanation for this sneak attack." Carlos stared back at her, his temperature rising. At that moment Nedra looked as tough and uncompromising as his mother.

"When did you decide to *volunteer* at the dinner?" Nedra gazed back at him and nodded as she watched his expression change. "So the fog is clearing?"

"Okay. Okay." Carlos felt like he'd just gotten a slap upside the head. He closed his office door and turned back to her.

"No, sweetie, it's not okay," Nedra snapped.

"Just hear me out. I wanted to tell you, but my mother… What I mean is…" He stopped and rubbed his face.

"You've got to be kidding me. You're thirty-five years old and the first thing you do is blame your mommy?"

Carlos held up both hands. "If you'd just calm down and let me explain."

"You ran to mommy after you got caught with drugs and guns. This story just gets better and better. I jumped into bed with a criminal and a mama's boy. I'm in the running for the Biggest Sucker of the Year award." Nedra squeezed her eyes shut.

"That's not fair, Nedra. Stop beating up on me a minute and let's talk." Carlos raised his voice and that got her attention.

Her eyes flew open. "Fine, Carlos, talk." She patted one foot as she looked at him.

"Let's sit down," he said in a quiet tone and pointed to the seating area. Nedra didn't move. "Please."

With a sniff, she marched over to the round table, pulled out a chair and sat down. "I can't wait to hear your explanation."

Carlos sat beside her and moved to put an arm around her shoulders, but she drew back sharply. He held up both palms. "Okay. Okay. How do I start?"

"With the first lie you told," Nedra tossed back.

"Part of my agreement with the DA was that I volunteer to fulfill two hundred hours of community service. They found marijuana and two hand guns hidden in the storeroom of my Easy Town shop. One of my employees had ties to the Forty-Sixth Street gang, but they couldn't prove that the drugs and guns belonged to him. My fingerprints were on the packages around them and this guy wouldn't talk. Since I had no previous record, and you should remember that, the DA was more than willing to let me do a diversion program." Carlos let out a deep sigh and sat back against his chair.

Nedra stared at him. "There's more."

"I had to give information about the cars that came through my shop. Apparently, drugs and guns were concealed in them. State troopers in Louisiana and Mississippi had been tracking these guys and finally made a traffic stop. They were driving those cars." Carlos relived the stab of fear he'd had when the police first questioned him and Brian.

"So they thought you were helping traffic drugs and guns. Were you?" Nedra raised an eyebrow.

"What? No, of course not!" Carlos huffed a few times to get his temper in check. "I've got too much to lose by doing something so stupid. Not even with my shops struggling to break even."

"Oh, so the cops thought you did it for extra money to keep up that lifestyle you're used to. Is that it?" Nedra sounded like a hardcore police interrogator.

"They're trained to follow all angles and to be suspicious, so yeah, they dug into my finances. I gave them as much help as I could." Carlos looked away.

"You knew or at least had an idea that your employee was shady." Nedra tilted her head to one side.

"No way, I would have fired his ass quick. But I kinda figured a few of the customers that rolled in were... urban entrepreneurs." He flinched as Nedra let out a sharp hiss.

"That's a cute way of saying you got cozy with street gangstas, Carlos. What the hell were you thinking? Wait; don't even answer because it's none of my business. I've known you for a month, so maybe I don't have the right to demand anything from you." Nedra closed her eyes again for a few seconds and then reopened them. "And your mother?"

"She advised me and talked to the assistant DA assigned to my case. That's all. No laws or rules were broken, but others might assume my mother put pressure on the DA to give me special treatment. That's not true," Carlos added quickly. "The diversion program is used a lot in cases like mine."

Nedra waved her hand. "Come on, Carlos. We both know your mother has pull in this parish with the city police, the sheriff's office and the DA."

"The DA's office wouldn't have gone along with it if I'd had a criminal background, or if they'd had evidence that I had a gang connection. I don't think you're being fair." Carlos looked at her, but Nedra wouldn't return his gaze.

She stared at the wall. "Why didn't you tell me the truth?"

He sighed and dropped his head. "My mother is in a very sensitive position when it comes to law enforcement. Not only does she have an election coming up, but she has future goals when it comes to her judicial career. She'd like to be considered for a federal judgeship in the next few years. Even a hint of scandal or talk of improper behavior as an officer of the court could kill her chances." He fidgeted as seconds ticked by with no reply.

"In other words, you didn't trust me not to run straight to Rod and tell him? Rod isn't running against your mother. He's going to run against..." Nedra's voice trailed off. "So the mayor got in on the act as well?"

"He and Brian's father grew up in the same neighborhood," he explained. "They were friends, like brothers really, practically all their lives. Brian was maybe eleven or twelve when his dad died. Mayor Bates promised him that he'd look after Brian."

Brian's father had been in a gang in the seventies and died from AIDS-related cancer following years of drug abuse. He had begged the mayor not to let Brian make the same mistakes. Carlos didn't feel right telling Nedra so much so soon. He pushed down the prick of guilt he felt at holding back, but Brian's story was not his to tell just yet.

"Okay, so you thought I'd go running to Rod to give him ammo to use against the mayor? I'm sure Judge Jacobs had an opinion when she found out about us," Nedra said quietly. She turned to Carlos.

"She doesn't know you." He put a hand on Nedra's shoulder. When she didn't pull away, he moved closer.

"Neither do you. Like I said, we've only known each other for a month," she replied, looking down at her hands folded in her lap.

"Do you really think I'm a drug dealer and gun runner, Nedra?" Carlos put his arm across the back of her chair. He tensed as moments passed.

"No, I don't. Do you trust me with this information?" Nedra twisted the strap of her purse between her fingers.

"Yes, I do. I would have told you everything eventually after the holidays." Carlos hugged her to him and rested his head against hers.

"Why would 'after the holidays' make a difference?" she asked, relaxing in his embrace.

"Because we'll still be together and planning our next Christmas."

He felt a surge of happiness when Nedra's reply was a tight hug and tears.

****

The next day, Nedra met her sisters and Maida for lunch at the Mall of Louisiana. They sat in La Madeleine's restaurant near a window with a view of the carousel. Kids squealed with delight as parents took pictures. Jarae and Gaylynn kept exchanging glances, while Maida just shook her head. All three were still digesting Nedra's revelations about Carlos. She told them that he'd had to do community service, but left out the part about the involvement of Mayor Bates.

"I melted when he talked about our future. You think he's pulled a fast one? Now that my romantic haze has cleared up, I'm wondering if I'm being stupid over a man *again*." Nedra picked over the salad she'd ordered to go with La Madeleine's famous French onion soup.

Jarae raised her professionally arched eyebrows at Nedra. "Carlos is known for being a real smooth operator. I hear some of his friends call him 'The Closer'. When nobody else can get to a woman, Carlos Jacobs can."

Gaylynn squinted at their older sister. "Gee, thanks

for being so supportive, Jay."

"Hey, don't ask if you don't want the truth." Jarae merely shrugged and took another bite of her chicken salad croissant.

"Listen, sounds to me like the guy is sincere. I mean, he introduced Nedra to his little girl and has spent practically every free moment with her," said Maida. She looked at Jarae, who shrugged again because her mouth was full.

"I agree with Maida. People can change. Besides, he wasn't caught with drugs or using them. You haven't heard about him using, huh?" Gaylynn glanced at Jarae again. "Okay, Ms. Twenty-four Hour News Channel."

Jarae swallowed and sipped from her glass of iced tea. She patted her lips with a fancy paper napkin. "I have to say, other than the typical smoking a little weed in college, I've never heard Carlos was into drugs."

"He smokes weed?" Maida squeaked. She flinched as heads turned and diners nearby stared. "Sorry."

"Thank you for putting us on blast," Nedra snapped.

"I didn't say he still does, girl. He played around in college like a lot of us. Just like we all got stinking drunk on cheap booze at least three times. Don't front 'cause you know I know," said Jarae, pointing at Maida and Gaylynn in turn.

Maida grinned. "Point made."

"But some forgot to stop partying and ended up addicted. I don't know now." Gaylynn frowned.

"You were just saying that he sounded sincere and that you believed him." Nedra blinked at Gaylynn.

"Evidence of past drug use and his association with drug dealers sounds bad." Gaylynn picked up her glass of pink lemonade and took a long pull on the straw, still frowning.

"I hate this. Just when I'm having the happiest Christmas in years, crap happens," said Nedra, pushing away her salad plate.

"Trust men to screw up everything. I'm telling you, we've been catching hell since Adam blamed Eve for everything." Maida nodded, as though dropping ageless wisdom on her friends. "Look at Imani."

"What happened with Imani and Errol?" gasped Jarae, dropping her croissant as though this latest gossip was way tastier.

"Imani kept looking until she found out what she didn't want to know," Maida replied. "Errol called her manipulative and a control freak. Said he'd tried to make it work, but he got tired of her following him around and going through his pockets. He went to his company's conference and met a woman who works at the Houston office. They hit it off and, long story short, he's transferring to Houston and they're dating."

Gaylynn gasped and put a hand over her heart. "Oh no, poor Imani."

Jarae shook her head slowly. "Umph, umph, umph."

"I haven't seen or heard from her since the day she was in my office," Nedra sighed.

"Imani did her usual thing; went overboard and smothered the man. I tried telling her, but she wasn't hearing it," Maida said.

"I'm going to give her a call." Gaylynn wore a look of sympathy for their friend.

"Call her cell. She went home to Mobile to be with her family for the holidays. At least she won't be feeling awful. They're very close and supportive." Maida sipped her diet cola with a thoughtful expression.

Nedra looked at the others. "We've got to get together with Imani when she's back in town."

"For sure," Jarae replied, and the women nodded in agreement.

Nedra bit her lower lip. "Imani was with Errol a lot longer than I've known Carlos."

"Okay, can we all agree that Imani has run off the last three men in her life?" Maida asked, leaning across the table, her voice low.

"At least," Gaylynn chimed in. "I hate to say it, but you're right. Once is bad luck. Twice is a bad decision. Three times is a trend."

"Maybe so, or Errol could have been making an excuse. You know, like Adam blaming Eve when the crap hit the fan. Guys will point the finger at you in a minute," argued Jarae, scowling at the world.

"He could have been honest with her, instead of slipping around." Nedra joined her older sister with her own scowl.

Maida put a hand on Nedra's arm. "Girl, we're not talking about Carlos."

"No, but we could be. We're talking about honesty and not keeping secrets," Nedra replied.

"Okay, we know what happened with Imani. Now let's examine this thing with Carlos. It's not just about him. His mother has her reputation on the line and asked him not to tell. Y'all know we'd all do whatever for our mamas. C'mon now," said Gaylynn, waving a hand.

"True that," Jarae replied. "And if one of my boys got in trouble, I'd take whatever steps necessary to keep them out of the system."

"Amen," Maida said with gusto.

Nedra felt the rock on her chest lift a bit. "Under the circumstances I would have done the same thing. Whew, this relationship stuff is complicated when you add family into the mix."

"Hey, if you have any lingering doubts, look him up. Your law-enforcement pals won't mind giving you the 411 when you tell them he's your new man." Jarae pointed a forefinger at Nedra. "Do a background check."

Nedra shook her head firmly as the other two clamored to agree with Jarae. "I'm not going down that road. We just talked about how Imani pushed Errol away by playing detective. I'm either going to trust what he tells me or not. My gut tells me to trust Carlos."

"Then that's settled. Let's share dessert." Jarae waved to the waiter as the others laughed at her.

Nedra grinned at her older sister. "Girl, trust you to keep your priorities straight."

## Chapter 10

Saturday night, Nedra and Carlos strolled along with Carly in the middle, each holding one of her hands as they moved through the crowd. New Roads looked like a nineteenth-century village. Strings of white lights decked all of the antique stores and specialty shops on Main Street. Other multicolored lights in the shapes of angels, bows and small Christmas trees hung from lamp posts. The cool night air and cozy small-town atmosphere had everyone in a good mood, it seemed.

"Come on, I hear music. I think the Christmas rollercoaster is this way," said Carly. Straining forward, she pulled the two adults along like a tiny tug boat guiding two larger vessels through a sea of people.

"Slow down sweet pea. We'll get there soon enough." Carlos laughed as he watched his daughter huff and puff with the effort to hurry them.

"I don't want to miss a seat. Look at all those kids trying to get there." Carly continued to march them towards the music. Her little red, knitted hat had a green pom-pom on the top, which bobbed as she moved.

Nedra smiled and increased her pace. "She's making sense, Carlos. It looks like everyone is headed for the same place. I say we step it up."

"Thank you, Miss Nedra. Now come on, daddy." Carly yanked Carlos' hand until he was even with them.

"All right, all right, I've been voted down. We head for the rides instead of window shopping."

Carlos scooped up Carly and soon his long legs had them making good progress. Nedra had to work hard to keep up. Within seconds she was out of breath, but they soon arrived at the roped-off entrance to the area with small carnival rides. More multicolored lights flashed. To the left was a section with bumper cars painted green, red, gold and purple. Just behind that, a merry-go-round had been set up. There were many booths with games of chance to win prizes and straight ahead was a large carousel. Reindeer, sleighs and elves rotated to music.

Carly dropped the adults' hands, and jumped up and down. "Daddy, I want to ride the big reindeer. Please, please. This way!"

Carlos grabbed her hand before she could race off. "Whoa. We have to get tickets first. I gotta admit you were right, baby girl. We beat a big crowd."

Even though they weren't too far down, they stood in line for twenty minutes. Carly's excitement grew as she watched other children smile with delight as they rode the carousel. She barely paid any attention to Carlos, who took the opportunity to whisper his plans to Nedra to wrap Carly's presents later, after she fell asleep.

"You'll have no problem wrapping them in peace. She's going to be exhausted." Nedra glanced around at the activity.

Carlos leaned close to Nedra and spoke close to her ear, "I promise you, within an hour of getting back to my place, Carly will be sound asleep. I'll just manage to give her a bath and brush her hair."

"You've got this parenting thing down. I salute you, sir." Nedra nudged him affectionately. "But brush her hair before bed?"

He nodded. "Carly likes her hair groomed and covered with a satin scarf before she goes to bed."

Nedra laughed. "Say what?"

"She has her beauty routine," he replied, laughing with her.

Nedra loved how his eyes sparkled when he talked about his little girl. No matter what Jarae may have heard, Carlos didn't look anything like a player when Carly was around. Instead, he was the loving father on a

Christmas greeting card. Nedra ticked off another important box: great father. She hooked her arm through one of his and felt like she was in one of those sentimental holiday commercials.

Slowly, the line moved forward until Carlos stepped up to the ticket stand. "We need three," he told the guy holding a roll of tickets.

"Three it is." The man counted them off.

"Wait a minute," said Nedra, tapping Carlos on the shoulder.

He looked at her. "You didn't think Carly would have all the fun, did you?"

"Yaay, daddy and Miss Nedra are gonna ride." Carly bounced around with delight. "C'mon!"

"B-but I- I mean," Nedra stammered as she was pulled towards the carousel. "I've never been on one of these things in my life."

"Now you'll be able to tell all your friends what you did over the holidays." Carlos winked at her and grinned. "Hey!"

Carly shot over to the motionless ride. Moments later, she stood next to Rudolph the Red-nosed Reindeer, after managing to beat three other kids to it. She had her arms around Rudolph's neck as Carlos and Nedra caught up with her.

"Girl, you were determined to get this reindeer, weren't you?" Carlos panted. He took a few breaths before he lifted her onto Rudolph's back. "She's even more competitive than her mother."

Nedra giggled as he rolled his eyes. "I'll take this little sleigh over here," she said.

Carlos nodded and stood next to Carly. Kids clamored to climb into the sleighs, hop on reindeers and slide into cars carved in the shape of Santa's elves. The music started and lights began to flash. A cheer went up as the carousel started slowly. Before she realized it,

Nedra was laughing and waving to the crowd with the others. Everyone sang along with the carols that played for the next few turns. All too soon, they slowed until the carousel stopped again.

Once they were back on solid ground, Carly clapped her hands. "I want to try the bumper cars next. Then may we please ride the merry-go-round again? Please, please?" She batted her thick, dark eyelashes up at Carlos.

"Sounds like a fun idea to me," Nedra chimed in. She imitated Carly and fluttered her eyelashes as well. "Pretty please, with butter-cream icing on top?"

"No need to beg, girls." Carlos kissed Carly and then Nedra.

For almost two hours they all had a blast and ended up taking every ride three times. Nedra earned Carly's admiration when she hit the target at a booth. They walked away with a cute, stuffed monkey, whom the little girl promptly named Marcus, and then bought corn dogs and lemonade at a food booth.

"Honey, where did you get that name?" asked Carlos, pointing to the stuffed animal.

"Mama dated Mr. Marcus for a little while, but then she didn't like him anymore. She called him a stupid monkey, who didn't have a decent job or the right friends. I sorta liked him though. He was funny." Carly related the account in a childish, matter-of-fact tone.

Nedra struggled not to choke on a mouthful of lemonade. She swallowed, and then took in and let out a deep breath. Her eyes watered from the need to laugh out loud.

Carlos sat with his eyes wide and his jaw open. He was obviously at a loss how to respond.

"Well, you did ask," Nedra finally managed to get out. Then she lost the battle and fell against Carlos, giggling so hard that she became weak.

Carly seemed unaware of the effect of her words. She happily ate her corndog and watched the action around them. They spent another few minutes finishing their food. When his daughter yawned for the third time and leaned against him, Carlos nodded a signal to Nedra.

They strolled through Christmas Village again, this time lingering to look into the windows, and Carly perked up for a while at the mechanical toys displayed. By the time they headed for the lot where Carlos had parked his SUV, Carly's eyes were fluttering as she tried to keep them open.

"This was a great idea," said Carlos. He lifted Carly up and carried her for the last few yards with her head resting on his shoulder.

Nedra smoothed down the girl's hair. "Yes, it was."

When they reached the Accura, Carlos placed Carly into the booster seat in the back. Her eyes were shut as she yawned once again. Nedra's heart filled with affection and warmth. This little taste of family life had kicked off dreams of making her own nest; a cute house, holiday dinners, and baking cupcakes for the kids to take to school.

"What did I tell you?" asked Carlos, as he closed the car door and pointed to Carly, who was fast asleep on the back seat. He was about to go on when his cell phone played a tune. He glanced at the caller ID and made a face before answering, "Hi, Mother."

"She's a concerned grandparent," Nedra whispered. She covered her mouth when he rolled his eyes.

"Say that again." Carlos transferred the cell phone to his right hand and put it to his ear again. "Slow down, okay? I don't know what you're talking about. No, Nedra wouldn't know."

Nedra blinked at him and mouthed the word, "What?" Judge Jacobs talked so loudly that Nedra could hear every word.

Carlos huffed and shook his head. He tried to get a word in a couple of times, but his mother rattled on in rapid-fire fashion.

"I'll look at it now. Fine, but…" Carlos looked shaken as he touched his phone and ended the call.

"Is your family okay? Is anyone sick or hurt?" Nedra's heart hammered at the expression on Carlos' face. Calls at night and loud voices didn't signal good news in her experience.

He frowned. "She said to look at the Channel Three website."

"I have their news app." Nedra took out her smartphone and tapped the screen twice. "I don't see-- damn!"

Carlos looked at the bold headline and opened the story.

"Sources allege that the mayor has been engaged in giving preferential treatment when awarding contracts. But the most damning claim is that the mayor personally intervened in criminal cases. According to reports, Mayor Bates has helped broker less severe sentences or no prosecution at all for politically connected individuals. One case cited was that of Carlos Jacobs, son of Judge Yvonne Jacobs."

Nedra put a hand over her mouth as he read the rest in silence. Carlos continued to stare at the phone after he reached the end of the article. The sound of laughter from the crowds around them faded.

She put a hand on his arm. "I'm so sorry, honey."

"Really, Nedra? Are you really sorry?" Carlos asked, handing her back the phone.

"You don't think I gave that story to the media? That's crazy." Nedra stared at him.

"You were furious that day."

"So you think my first instinct was to call a reporter? Are you serious?" Nedra went from sympathetic to angry in two seconds. "How dare you."

"By the way, you never told me how you found out," he said. "It's real common these days for folks to do background checks on each other while they're dating. Did you do a little investigating?" Carlos crossed his arms and stared back at Nedra.

Nedra glanced at the car to confirm that Carly had drifted off to sleep, and spoke low. "No, I didn't, but you shouldn't have even asked that question."

He squinted at her. "Okay, then how did this get out?"

"The bigger question, Carlos, is why you're so quick to accuse me of outing you and your mama. I thought you knew me better." Nedra grew more outraged by the minute.

"This is a twofer for your boss. He gets to slam his future political opponent and get back at my mother. I'm guessing you vented about me to the good constable. He was probably patting you on the shoulder with one hand and dialing his reporter pals with the other." Carlos paced beside the car as he spoke. "My mother was right. I should have been more careful."

"Okay, so your mama warned you about me. Well, I'm not surprised." Nedra forgot about being supportive, and she definitely didn't feel a need to defend herself.

Carlos stood still and faced her again. "What exactly does that mean?"

"She probably said something about me working for the enemy. I don't even need to ask. Well, my boss happens to be an upright kind of guy. He doesn't expect me to engage in political dirty work, and I wouldn't even if he did," Nedra snapped.

"He doesn't expect you to do it because he's so good at doing his own political dirty work. You're either naive or in serious denial," Carlos snorted.

"Don't blame me if your mother has a big target on

her chest. She's not exactly considered Miss Congeniality downtown," she shot back.

Carlos breathed in and out a few times. "Okay, I think it's time for me to take you home, for real."

"Fine." Nedra marched to the passenger side and got in. She didn't slam the door only because she didn't want to scare Carly out of a sound sleep.

The drive back to Baton Rouge seemed to last for three hours rather than thirty minutes. The night might have been pleasantly chilly, but inside the Accura the temperature hovered just above freezing. When they finally arrived at Nedra's apartment, she got out of the car without speaking.

"Nedra, wait a minute." Carlos glanced at the backseat. Satisfied that Carly was still asleep, he got out. "Look, we both went a bit overboard. I wasn't accusing you of deliberately stabbing me in the back."

"Hmm, I kinda remember that's exactly what you did." Nedra raised an eyebrow at him.

"Okay, so maybe you were upset and confided in someone at the office, like your boss?" Carlos stood in waiting mode.

"No, I didn't. Next." Nedra folded her arms and studied him.

"I just want to know how you found out," Carlos said.

"Why, so your powerful mother and the mayor can exact revenge? I'll bet Mama Judge is sharpening up her gavel to come after me. Go home, Carlos. I'm sure she's waiting for your report." She started to turn away when he caught her arm.

"Don't act stupid. If you tell me how the story got out then I can…"

Nedra shook his hand from her arm. "Right, you'll move the rest of the skeletons to another closet. I'm not the stupid one, Carlos. And, just so you know, Judge

Jacobs is welcome to investigate me. No secrets to broadcast I'm afraid. Goodnight."

"I didn't say you were stupid. Nedra, wait." Carlos began to follow her, but stopped when she spun around.

"I think you need to take the night off trying to explain anything to me." Nedra marched up to her front door, unlocked it and went in.

****

Sunday morning, Nedra lay in bed with her down comforter pulled up to her nose. She would think about getting up and then talk herself out of it. Nedra hadn't slept very well and now she had a monster headache. When her doorbell rang, she groaned and placed both hands over her face. Maybe she was just imagining the cheerful chiming. It went off again. She groaned even louder and got up.

"Okay, Lord, you're punishing me because I didn't go to church," Nedra grumbled as she marched to the front door and looked through the peephole. Her mother gazed back at her.

"I know you're standing on the other side of this door. Now open up," Darcie Lee said. She still wore her church clothes: a navy blue suit and matching, wide-brimmed hat.

Nedra hurriedly undid the locks, swung the door wide and hugged her. "Good morning, Mama. Come on in."

"Uh-huh. You look a mess. Gaylynn told me about the fight with Carlos, and how you and she stayed up until three o'clock this morning talking. And, yes, I know about the report. I saw it on the news last night."

Darcie Lee put down a box, kicked off her shoes, and then took off her church hat and jacket. She walked into Nedra's kitchen and started making coffee as she talked. Once she had the brewing in progress, she opened the refrigerator.

"Gaylynn needs to keep her big mouth shut." Nedra sat down on one of the three stools at her breakfast counter.

"I'll talk to her about that one of these days," Darcie Lee replied.

"Sure you will, right about the time pigs fly. You love getting all the news you can use." Nedra breathed in the wonderful smell of coffee brewing. "Why aren't you enjoying Sunday brunch with your friends?"

"Because my child needs me."

Her mother put four slices of whole wheat bread into the toaster. Nedra started several times to stop her, but didn't. The truth was she felt better having her mother there to listen.

Darcie Lee took a small skillet down from a hook, wiped it and cracked open some eggs into it. Humming a gospel song, she cooked up two plates of breakfast with the practiced ease of a skilled chef. Along with the small cinnamon buns from the box she'd brought and two cups of coffee, she prepared a tasty meal for two.

Darcie Lee placed one serving in front of Nedra. She then sat down with her own plate, said grace, and sipped her coffee. "Eat. You'll get sick being miserable on an empty stomach." She took a dainty bite of toast. "Now, tell Mama about it."

"Not much to tell. The story came out, Judge Jacobs thinks I'm the source, and I got into a big fight with Carlos." Nedra tasted a small bit of scrambled egg.

"So the story is true about him getting arrested? That doesn't sound good. You know how I feel about you girls dating thugs." Darcie Lee shook her head and sipped her coffee.

"Carlos isn't a thug, Mama. Some drug dealers tried to use his business to commit their crimes. I don't believe Carlos was involved at all." Nedra realized her mother was regarding her with both eyebrows raised.

Darcie Lee patted her lips with a napkin. "You sound like his defense lawyer. Okay, so his mama is convinced you talked to the media. Why?"

"He didn't actually volunteer at the Holiday Hospitality Thanksgiving dinner. He was doing community service as part of a plea deal. I found out on Friday and confronted Carlos about keeping secrets from me." Nedra pushed the eggs around on her plate.

"Judge Jacobs doesn't believe in coincidences. I can see her point." Darcie Lee shrugged when her daughter huffed and puffed. "Well then, who talked?"

Nedra sighed and put her fork down.

Her mother calmly ate a slice of toast and half her eggs.

"Well, Dwayne Grover told me about Carlos."

"The mayor's special assistant?" Darcie Lee tilted her head to one side.

"He's been trying to get a date with me. A little thing like marriage doesn't stop old Dwayne from running after women. I let him know I wasn't interested at all and his ego couldn't take it." Nedra scowled just thinking about him.

"So he gets the dirt on Carlos to get back at you. To top it off, he talks to reporters. He's a real lowdown man." Darcie Lee snorted in disgust.

Nedra brushed her hair from her cheek and shook her head. "No, Mama, that doesn't make sense. Dwayne is just as ambitious as the mayor. He wouldn't talk to the reporters about something that could bounce back on his boss."

"But he just couldn't resist tossing a bomb at you to mess up what you have with Carlos." Darcie Lee chewed and thought. "So, if Dwayne didn't talk to the reporters, then who?"

Nedra groaned and placed both hands over her face. "A few minutes after Dwayne left, Rod walked out of his office.

"Politics is a contact sport, sweetie." Darcie Lee ate the last of her toast. "Now what?"

Nedra drained her coffee cup and put it down. "I don't know."

Darcie Lee straightened up the kitchen despite Nedra's objections. Then she retrieved her jacket, hat and shoes. Seconds after going into Nedra's half bath, she emerged looking like the proper church lady again.

"You two need to talk this out," she said. "Yes, I know, I'm no Yvonne Jacobs fan either, but her son treated you with love and respect. And you're miserable, which means you love him." She kissed her daughter's forehead. "The next few days will tell."

"Tell what?" asked Nedra, trudging behind her mother to the front door.

"If you're going to let that little weasel Dwayne ruin what you two kids have. Are you going to give him exactly what he wanted?" Darcie Lee faced Nedra, her purse hanging primly from the crook of one arm.

"Darcie Lee Morgan Wallace, you know exactly what to say." Nedra hugged her fiercely.

## Chapter 11

Carlos kissed the top of Carly's head and watched her race back to the Santa's Toy Shop display at the Mall of Louisiana. Monday, Christmas Eve, and the place was packed with last-minute shoppers. He tried to let the laughter around him penetrate his dark mood, but it wasn't happening. At least Carly seemed not to notice. Luckily, she was too young to care about the news, other than reports of Santa sightings.

Local television weathermen were pretending to track Santa's sleigh moving towards Louisiana, but Carlos and his parents paid more attention to reports of political corruption in the mayor's office. The Baton Rouge media seemed thrilled to have such a story in what was usually a slow news cycle.

Childish squeals of delight jerked him out of his grim reverie. Carlos watched as Carly and at least ten other kids rode a miniature train. She waved at him as the little red car she rode in made a turn around the track. He envied the carefree days of childhood and waved back. Then he spotted his business partner wading through the crowd of shoppers. When Brian looked up from his cell phone, Carlos waved to him as well.

"Hey, man. Doing your last-minute dash for presents, huh?" Carlos laughed when his friend grimaced.

"I'm telling you, bru, this stuff sucks." Brian huffed out his frustration. Then he grinned and held up the shopping bags he held in one hand. "Luckily, this hot saleslady took me under her wing. Got everybody covered, except my uncle, and I got her phone number, too. Merry Christmas, baby."

Carlos shook his head. "I thought you were spending Christmas with one or both of the twins."

"That was Saturday night, man; now it's time to move on. Shelia is an older lady in her forties. She's a perfect combination; a widow with a decent job and no kids at home. I bet she can cook, too." Brian nodded.

"Daddy, look," Carly called out. She rode in the engine car of the train, turning a little steering wheel.

Carlos waved at her. "Good job, baby girl."

"You're still doing the family man thing, I see. Where is Ms. Right?" Brian glanced around.

"We hit a big bump after that story came out." Carlos gazed at Carly as she continued to have fun.

"Damn, that was cold. So you think she snitched?" asked Brian. "I mean, you told me how mad she was at you for not telling her. Then the story hit the street. That's a big coincidence if you ask me."

"I think her boss got curious about me and tapped his sources downtown to find out. I just don't believe Nedra would have gone to reporters." Carlos had repeated this theory to his parents at least a dozen times in the last twenty-four hours.

Brian seemed to read his thoughts. "I'll bet your mama ain't buyin' it."

"Yeah, well." Carlos rubbed his jaw and sighed.

"Look, I better head off. I'm going to pick up this electric car for Bradley. My aunt and sister have been on my back about not spending enough time with my kids. Humph, they always got something to say. Never mind that me working hard helps pay their doggone bills." Brian snorted. "I deserve some fun, too."

"Right." Carlos didn't bother arguing. He accepted Brian for who he was: self-absorbed and he spent a lot of time pursuing his brand of fun. "Kids need attention more than material things."

"I'll explain that to the family court judge next time their mamas demand more child support. Let's see how far that gets me." Brian gave a cynical laugh. He glanced at his cell phone. "I gotta go, bru. I'm treating Shelia to lunch."

"Hmm? Oh yeah, right. See you later."

Carlos noticed that Brian was wearing an expensive, black cashmere sweater. His partner seemed suddenly flush with cash for shopping. A phrase from the news article about his shop and the police raid popped into Carlos' head. *The police suspected more employees were involved in concealing the drugs and guns.*

"No, I'm getting way too paranoid," he told himself.

The investigation linked only one of the shop employees to the scheme. But how could he have gained access to the shop so often without being seen? Carlos watched his friend and business partner stride away. Then he took out his cell phone and made a call to a fraternity brother, who happened to be a successful private investigator.

****

On Christmas Eve, Nedra was in her office waiting. She knew Rod would be in because he'd told her so. Tapping one of her favorite ink pens on the desktop, she glanced through a few files. Hearing footsteps, she felt certain it was him. Only a couple of security officers roamed the halls and they had already made their hourly walk through. She left her office, went to his door, and knocked.

"Come in." Rod looked up as Nedra opened the door. "Why, it's my super-dedicated assistant. I thought you took today off, along with most of the folks in this building."

"I did. Can we talk?" she asked, closing the door.

"Sure. Have a seat. I can make us some hot chocolate." Rod started to rise.

"No thanks. I'm going to get right to the point. Did

you release the story about Carlos?" Nedra asked, sitting down across from him.

Rod settled back in his red-leather executive chair. He wore a somber expression and rested both hands on the desktop. "The story wasn't about Carlos, Nedra. It was about the mayor's abuse of power. The print article was long, and the example involving your boyfriend was only a couple of paragraphs."

Nedra held her temper in check, but barely. "Okay, now back to my question."

"I understand you're upset…"

"You're so right I'm upset, sir. Okay, that little newsflash has caused problems between us, but his little girl is in town for Christmas." Nedra frowned at him.

"I didn't know, but…"

"The diversion program is used with people who don't have a previous criminal record." Nedra's anger started to pick up steam. "Naturally, none of that was mentioned by the reporters on television or in the paper."

Constable Davidson cut in before Nedra could speak again. "I said the article wasn't about Carlos Jacobs. Let me finish. As you've figured out, I heard Dwayne's little speech the other day. But no, I didn't rush to the media."

Nedra raised an eyebrow. "Then how did it get out?"

"I won't pretend to be a saint, Nedra. I could have used the information in my campaign. I did discuss it with my strategy team. Obviously, one of them jumped the gun. I wouldn't have released this information so far ahead of the election. I'm sorry the story hurt your relationship with the young man.

"Carlos wasn't convicted of a crime and there was no evidence that he did anything wrong. But now it looks like he's a thug who got off because his mother is a judge." Nedra twisted her hands together.

Constable Davidson got up from his desk and walked around to sit in the chair next to Nedra. "My intention is not to hurt Carlos. But Judge Jacobs, the mayor and their pals have been misusing their positions. By the way, the *Daily News* investigative reporter has been digging for months. She contacted me back in September. I wouldn't be surprised if she already knew about Carlos."

"My mother is right. She told me politics is a contact sport. So you're going to go after Judge Jacobs?" Nedra gazed at her boss.

"If she is involved in questionable activities then her name will be mentioned. I'll let Carlos know you had nothing to do with that story coming out, though he may not believe me." He gave Nedra a paternal pat on the arm and went back to sit at his desk.

She frowned. "No thanks. If we don't survive this, maybe it wasn't meant to be. I should arrange for Dwayne's boss to find out he talked to me."

Rod lifted one dark eyebrow and a slow smile lit up his face. "Go for it."

"But..." Nedra thought about Dwayne's smarmy expression. She smiled back at her boss and headed to her office.

****

Later that afternoon at her apartment, Nedra joined her sisters to wrap gifts. The annual tradition had started six years earlier with Jarae and Gaylynn hiding their children's toys at their sister's house. The smell of freshly baked cookies and brewed coffee filled the air, but the holiday scents and sounds had no affect on Nedra's mood. The sisters' usual lively banter as they put together parts and wrestled ribbons was subdued.

"Well, look at the bright side," Jarae said as she sipped from her mug of pumpkin spice coffee.

Gaylynn stopped in the act of taking another bite out of a gingerbread man cookie. "There's a bright side to losing the best boyfriend you've ever had on Christmas Eve?"

Nedra looked at her younger sister. "Gee, thanks for making sure I remember why I'm so depressed."

Gaylynn winced. "Sorry, I should have worded that differently."

"You should have kept your mouth shut," Jarae retorted. "As I was saying, the good thing is you won't have the in-laws from hell. Close your eyes and imagine family holiday dinners sitting across from Judge Jacobs and her hubby. Five bucks says when you open your eyes you'll be feeling a lot better."

Nedra burst out laughing in spite of her blue mood. "You're insane, Jarae."

"I'm talking about a blessing in disguise. You won't have to deal with some other mess with 'Da Judge'." Jarae put down her mug and started wrapping a boxed set of toy cars.

"I suppose it could be for the best that it happened this early in our relationship," Nedra replied.

Nedra sure didn't feel like she was on 'the bright side'. At that moment it felt like the worst of all possible scenarios. She heaved a sigh and blinked back a tear. The sisters continued to wrap toys in silence for another ten minutes while Nedra sat staring at a cute baby doll that was for Misha. The Christmas she'd looked forward with Carlos and Carly had gone up in smoke.

Finally, Jarae stood and marched over to the coffee table. She snatched up Nedra's cell phone. "Here. Call him." She held out the phone inches from her sister's nose.

"I agree," Gaylynn piped up. "You've let out about fifteen gloomy sighs in the last hour. I've been keeping count."

"What about the 'blessing in disguise' talk?" Nedra gazed at the phone in hope, but still didn't touch it.

"Pure bull to try and make you feel a little less horrible. Don't give douche-bag Dwayne or Judge Wicked Witch the satisfaction. Besides, a good man is hard to find."

"She's right, Nedra. You owe it to yourself to at least try. Love will find a way," said Gaylynn. Setting the toy in her lap aside, she put her arm around her sister's shoulder.

Nedra took the phone and wiped a tear from her cheek. "I have the best sisters in the known universe."

"I have to agree," Gaylynn joked and then giggled.

"And if you tell mama I said she was right about something, I'll slap you into next Christmas." Jarae pointed a finger at Nedra and went back to her task of putting a huge, red bow on a present for her youngest.

"My lips are sealed." Nedra hugged them both and then walked into her bedroom. She hesitated a few seconds before dialing. Carlos answered on the first ring.

\*\*\*\*

Carlos paced around his living room. Glancing at the clock on his smartphone, he made another lap around the sofa. He looked out the window and then went to arrange a few items on a bookshelf. Clearing his throat, he stood straight.

"I never should have even assumed you leaked that story. Forgive me for being a stupid fool. I'm sorry and you can slap me if you want for being a suspicious slug." Carlos rubbed his forehead. "Sounds appropriately apologetic, with a touch of groveling."

He shook his head slowly. The last twenty-four hours had been lonely without Nedra. His mother had tried to tell Carlos he'd get over her. But if the past day had been any indication, he didn't intend to test his mother's theory. He missed Nedra's smile and the way he felt when she was beside him. Why stretch out that kind of misery? Carlos knew what he wanted.

The doorbell rang and his heart thumped. Taking a deep breath, he opened the front door. The beat in his chest picked up rapidly when he looked at the vision standing before him. Nedra looked stunning in a deep-red, cowl-neck sweater, blue jeans and tan boots.

"Hi." She nodded, but didn't move.

Carlos couldn't stop himself, and he didn't want to. He pulled Nedra into his arms and kissed her hard. He kissed her eyes, her forehead and then tasted her lips again. Nedra held still for a few moments and then melted into him.

"Ooo-wee, that's some strong mistletoe you got, neighbor."

They looked up to see the elderly man from the condo across the driveway grinning at them.

Nedra blushed and straightened her sweater. "I think we've made somebody's day."

"Better come inside so we can continue this discussion." Carlos grinned and gave his neighbor a thumbs-up gesture.

Once he closed the door, Nedra spun him around and gave him her version of a passionate greeting. Her mouth closed over his for a long, delicious time. Carlos no longer had a reason to hold back. He rubbed her body until he became dazed with desire. Then they stepped away from each other.

"Whew." Nedra fanned herself.

"Yeah."

Carlos reached for her again, but Nedra shook her head. "Let's talk before we get caught up again." She walked to the bar separating the kitchen from the living room, and sat down.

He followed and took the bar stool next to her. He took both of her hands in his. "I missed you so much.

Believe it or not, I was about to call you."

"It doesn't matter who called first. I wanted… no, I needed to see you. I'm not sure we can work out the whole political rivalry with your mother and my boss, but…" Nedra stopped when Carlos put a finger on her lips.

"I'm sure enough for both of us, Nedra. Slap me," he blurted out.

She blinked rapidly. "Say what?"

He started laughing and couldn't stop for a few seconds. Nedra caught the contagion and giggled along with him. They became helpless for a time, leaning against one another. Every time Carlos tried to speak, they dissolved into giggles once more. Finally, they got all of the tension and mirth released.

Nedra rested her forehead against his. "We're both out of our minds," she said. "Now tell me again that I should slap you."

"That was part of the speech I practiced. I was going to beg your forgiveness for acting a fool and invite you to slap me." Carlos kissed the end of her nose.

Nedra grinned at him. "I'll take a rain check on the slap. You might mess up again and then I'll need it."

"No way." Carlos grew serious. "I'm not going to do anything to make you want to tell me goodbye. I'm sorry for even thinking you talked to reporters about me."

"I know, honey, but you weren't being unreasonable. I would have been suspicious of that coincidence." Nedra took in a deep breath and let it out. "Dwayne Grover told me you were doing community service. I blew off his slimy attempts to hook up and he got ticked off."

"Slimy describes him exactly." Carlos wore a grimace of contempt.

"Ah, but what goes around comes around. Dwayne didn't do his homework." Nedra crossed her arms

"Huh?" Carlos sat back and looked at her.

"Dwayne was so excited to get back at me that he didn't get the whole story, including the part about Mayor Bates getting involved." Nedra nodded slowly as Carlos gasped.

"Damn, that was a dumb move. He needs to sharpen his investigative skills." Carlos shook his head and then started laughing again. "Did you?"

"I sure did. Now Mayor Bates knows his confidential assistant has a big mouth and that he's an idiot who spilled the goods on his own boss. Boom!" Nedra winked at Carlos.

"I would love to see a video of the mayor meeting with dumb Dwayne." Carlos shook his head and chuckled. Then he grew serious again. "Speaking of being sold out by someone you trust, Brian, my good friend and business partner, almost destroyed my business."

"How?"

"He let those gangstas use my shops to move guns and drugs. They paid him off big time. Brian made them think I knew all about his side hustle. They thought I got off because of my mother." Carlos pounded a fist on the marble counter of the bar. "He didn't even try to deny it. He said, 'Dude, I knew your mama wouldn't let us go to lock up; we're set'."

"Is he nuts? Now y'all are on the law-enforcement radar. He can't slide back into doing street biz with those guys." Nedra put a hand on her chest.

"I can't lie. I knew Brian had a shady side, but I didn't think he'd stab me in the back. Not when it came to the business and him knowing what those shops meant to me." Carlos shook his head and sat down.

"He's your partner, so now what?"

"As of this morning, he's out. He signed an agreement relinquishing his limited partnership. I don't even want to know where he got the twenty thousand he invested back in 2004."

Nedra rubbed Carlos' shoulder. "I'm so sorry you had to find out this way and buy him out."

"Buy him out? Hell, no. I didn't tell the police or, worse, my mother. That's the only payment he'll get from me. Brian wasn't sorry either, except for being caught and losing his other income stream." Carlos still felt the sting of betrayal.

"At least you know the truth and he won't take advantage of you again." Nedra hugged him. "Christmas is going to be a little grim, huh?"

Carlos pulled free and grabbed both of her hands. "No way, baby. Okay, our sleigh ride has been bumpy for the last few days…"

"To say the least," Nedra replied with a snort.

"But we still have reasons to be joyful. Carly is curious about the dinner tomorrow, so after she drags me out of bed at the crack of dawn, we'll show up for duty. Then I'll meet your family and you can come and meet mine."

"I don't know, Carlos. Maybe we should wait until after the holidays. I mean your parents." Nedra winced.

"They'll be polite when we visit and that's all I expect. I'll deal with them long term." Carlos hooked an arm around Nedra's neck and kissed her forehead. "People say I'm just like her. So when I decide what I want, folks had best get out of my way."

She grinned at him. "I'm scared of you, Mr. Jacobs."

"You won't have to deal with my mother. I'll get that straight from word go. Now let's get to wrapping presents." Carlos laughed when Nedra gave him a playful punch on the arm. "Ouch, woman."

"You're unbelievable. You mean to tell me you haven't done that yet?"

Carlos held up both hands. "I had a few things on

my mind, you know."

"Put on some Christmas music, and get out the gift wrap and ribbons. I'll make some hot chocolate with marshmallows," said Nedra, heading into the kitchen.

Carlos executed a sharp salute. "Yes, ma'am. You say 'Jump' and I don't ask why. I just ask how high. Since it's turned so cold, I'll light the fireplace. I have extra rolls of gift wrap in my car."

"Well, go get them then." Nedra waved at him as though shooing him out the door.

"Will do. Don't bother searching for your gift. It's too well hidden." Carlos grabbed his jacket from the hall closet.

Nedra glanced around the living. "Hmm, it never even crossed my mind."

They spent the next few hours enjoying the warmth that didn't come from the fireplace. Carlos savored being with Nedra and anticipating picking up Carly to spend the rest of their Christmas Eve together.

****

Nedra sighed with contentment as she looked around the dining room full of people. She had helped to serve the food, along with three-dozen other volunteers. The Christmas dinner coordinator had done an excellent job.

Carlos and Carly waved at her from across the wide room. They pushed a cart together, loaded with sweet potato and pecan pie slices on dessert plates. Nedra waved back and headed to the kitchen. Alice Faye was in full mode, giving orders with the crisp efficiency of a military leader, and she grinned when she noticed Nedra.

Alice Faye wiped her hands dry on a paper towel and tossed it into the trash. "Well, I'm glad to see you and that fine-looking man are still together," she said, nudging Nedra in the side with an elbow. "His little girl is as sweet as honey and such pretty manners, too."

"Carly is a doll." Nedra smiled as Alice Faye's grin grew wider. "Yes, and so is her daddy. Satisfied?"

"Love and happiness; that's what Christmas is all about," said Alice Faye, looking past her. She dropped her voice and leaned closer. "The mayor just walked in. This should be interesting."

Nedra turned to follow her gaze. The mayor gave Constable Davidson a stiff handshake, stood alongside him for a photo and then moved on. Dwayne trailed after him.

"I didn't think he'd make a scene," said Nedra. "They'll slug it out during the election. The gloves will come off."

"I'll hide the knives, just in case." Alice Faye giggled at her own joke. She clearly enjoyed the political drama and intrigue. "I hear Dwayne just barely hung on to his job, but only because his father and the mayor go way back. Dwayne is just a glorified gofer, from what I hear. But I'm not trying to spread gossip." Alice Faye watched her subjects mingle with other local officials.

"Of course not." Nedra chuckled.

Dwayne glanced at her, and turned sharply to head in the opposite direction.

"Well one good thing came out of the whole mess. Dwayne is going to stay away from me," she added.

Alice Faye craned her neck to follow the mayor as he continued his circuit of the room. "What?"

"Nothing. Good job as usual, Alice Faye. Merry Christmas." Nedra gave her a hug.

"Same to you, sweetheart," she replied, pecking Nedra on the cheek and scurrying off.

Carlos approached with a couple and two children. Carly skipped along beside them. "Hey, I want you to meet some of my family. This is my sister, Brianne, her husband and their kids Lincoln and Cheyenne. Family, this is Nedra Wallace."

"Pleased to meet you and Merry Christmas," replied Nedra. She shook hands with the adults and smiled at the children.

"We decided to stop by on the way to my mother-in-law's house. Carlos told us so much about the dinner. Maybe next year we'll volunteer," Brianne said.

Carlos beamed at them. "That's a great idea. We can make it a family affair."

"Miss Nedra, I'm going to be on television. A reporter interviewed me." Carly bounced up and down in anticipation.

"That's wonderful," said Nedra, giving the girl a congratulatory hug.

"We better get going. See y'all tonight," Brianne added.

Nedra and Carlos waved goodbye to them. Then she turned to him. "So the plan is that we help clean up here and head to my mama's house. They're so excited to meet you two."

"I saved room for more dressing. I love dressing." Before they could answer, Carly darted over off. "Miss Alice Faye, I can help. Let me."

The cook looked to Carlos for direction. When he nodded, she put a hand on Carly's shoulder. "Okay, sweetie. They're clearing the tables, so you take the trash off the trays and throw them in these big garbage cans."

"Yes, ma'am." Carly wore a look of concentration as she worked.

"She's serious about her work." Nedra laughed.

"And she'll be just as serious about having fun later on," Carlos replied. Then he moved closer to Nedra and whispered, "So will I."

Nedra gazed into his dark brown eyes and felt so much joy that she couldn't put it into words at thatmoment. She brushed her lips across his mouth.

"Merry Christmas, baby."

# ∼ About the Author ∼

Mix knowledge of voodoo, Louisiana politics and forensic social work with the dedication to write fiction while working each day as a clinical social worker, and you get a snapshot of author Lynn Emery. Lynn has been a contributing consultant to the magazine *Today's Black Woman* for three articles about contemporary relationships between black men and women. For more information visit:

**Visit me on the web at:**

www.lynnemery.com

**Connect with me on:**
**Twitter:** www.twitter.com/LEmeryWriter
**Facebook:** www.facebook.com/lynn.emery.author